Mosquito

Akhmet Baitursynov

Mosquito

Akhmet Baitursynov

Translated by
Jake Zawlacki

ACADEMIC STUDIES PRESS

BOSTON

2026

Library of Congress Cataloging-in-Publication Data

Names: Baĭtūrsynov, Akhmet, 1873–1937 author | Zawlacki, Jake translator | Baĭtūrsynov, Akhmet, 1873–1937. Mesa. | Baĭtūrsynov, Akhmet, 1873–1937. Mesa. English

Title: Mosquito / Akhmet Baitursynov; translated by Jake Zawlacki.

Description: Boston : Academic Studies Press, 2026. | Series: Central Asian literature in translation

Identifiers: LCCN 2025047812 (print) | LCCN 2025047813 (ebook) | ISBN 9798897831104 (paperback) | ISBN 9798897831111 (adobe pdf) | ISBN 9798897831128 (epub)

Subjects: LCGFT: Poetry

Classification: LCC PL76.9.B354 M4713 2026 (print) | LCC PL76.9.B354 (ebook)

LC record available at https://lccn.loc.gov/2025047812
LC ebook record available at https://lccn.loc.gov/2025047813

ISBN 9798897831104 (paperback)
ISBN 9798897831111 (adobe pdf)
ISBN 9798897831128 (epub)

Book design by Kryon Publishing Services
Cover design by Ivan Grave

Published by Academic Studies Press
1007 Chestnut Street
Newton, MA 02464, USA
press@academicstudiespress.com
www.academicstudiespress.com

Contents

Acknowledgements — vii

Introduction — ix

Translator's Note — xv

References — xxi

Mosquito — 2

Author's Note — 4

A Writer's Joy — 6

To My Kin — 8

From Zhadovskaya — 10

Khoja Nasreddin's Cunning — 12

Invitation to Study — 14

Năbek's Horse — 18

The Unlucky Peasant — 23

Geese — 29

The Ass and the Owl — 36

Kazakhness — 42

Kazakh Culture — 45

Letter to a Friend — 47

Pieces, Gathered — 53

Letter to My Mother — 60

My Prayer — 65

Words of the Captive — 70

A Farmer of Humanity   73

To the Blue Asses   76

To the City of Qa------   79

To My People   81

To Calm   85

To Mrs. N. K.   90

To My Little Brother Poet   94

Letter From My Brother-in-Law, I. B.   98

Reply to a Letter   103

Science   108

From Nadson   112

Garden   116

Pushkin's Voltaire   119

Horse   121

The Death of Alek the Wise   127

The Fisherman and the Fish   138

The Golden Rooster   155

From Lermontov   170

Acknowledgements

Versions of "Author's Note" and "To My People" first appeared in *Alchemy*.
A version of "Horse" first appeared in *Mantis*.
A version of "Kazakhness" first appeared in *Asymptote*.
A version of "Garden" first appeared in *Guernica*.
Versions of "A Writer's Joy" and "Words of the Captive" first appeared in the *Antonym*.

This book in your hands exists because of the contributions of Troy Zawlacki, Valerie Burgess, Nicholas Garza, Olivia Shoup, Scott and Adriana Hasser, Kevin Powers, Evelyn Kirkley, Dennis Keen, Marina Abrams, Robert Crews, William Smith, James Rooney, Tina Lim, Evan Alterman, Maira Serik, Azharuddin, Daniel Sheehan, Isaiah Whisner, Halina Duraj, and the many additional supporters on Kickstarter.

I wouldn't have embarked on this translation if it wasn't for the help of Symbat Nartay, Ariel Francisco, and Sophia Syltanqan. Their assistance was absolutely essential in not only fine-tuning translations, but giving me the confidence to lend my own voice to Akhmet. This project owes thanks to Sacha Idell for his assurance, Cooper Raterink for his ingenuity, Amina Kosbayeva for her support, Rafi Kopacz for his artistry, Dr. Steven Sabol for his expertise, and Erica Zawlacki for her kindness. Furthermore, I am very grateful to those at Academic Studies Press who have helped to hone this book into the absolute best version it can be.

I would also like to acknowledge that I wouldn't be where I am today if it wasn't for the endless patience of my Kazakh-language teachers, Sofia Syltanqan in Mongolia, Gulnara Glowacki at University Wisconsin-Madison, and Fatima Moldashova at Stanford University. Lastly, I'd like to thank Dr. John Fendrick, an incredible man and teacher who inspired a lifelong fascination with language.

Introduction

Akhmet Baitursynov (1872–1937) was a Kazakh poet, linguist, educator, politician, and nationalist active at the turn of the century and during the early years of the USSR. Born in Torghaĭ oblast, what is now the Qostanaĭ region of Kazakhstan, he received a traditional Islamic education and learned Arabic, Farsi, Ottoman Turkish, and Russian. In 1895, Baitursynov graduated from Orenburg Teacher's College, found a teaching position, and published his first article in a local newspaper.[1] As a teacher, he was heavily influenced by Ybyraĭ Altynsarin, a pedagogue who stressed teaching in both Russian and Kazakh.[2] After moving to the countryside to teach, a lifelong endeavor that earned him the title *Ūlt Ūstazy* (Teacher of the Nation),[3] he returned to Qostanaĭ and met the Russian Alexandra Ivanovna. They were soon married in an Islamic ceremony, Ivanovna having converted to Islam, and the bride took the name Badrisafa Mūkhamedsadyk Baitursynova.

In 1907, Baitursynov criticized the tsarist administration and was imprisoned for the first time; but his anti-colonial sentiments stemmed from his childhood. At the age of thirteen, he watched his father and brothers fight the Russian colonel Yakovlev as the colonel initiated a conflict with the Kazakh villagers. As punishment for this act of resistance, Baitursynov's father and brothers were exiled to Siberia for fifteen years.[4] Baitursynov himself was imprisoned once more in 1909 for similar reasons, after which he was exiled and moved to Orenburg.

It was during this period that Baitursynov began writing in earnest, and quickly gained renown for his translation of Ivan Krylov's book of fables *Forty Fables* (1909), which he adapted to harmonize with Kazakh culture, before beginning work on *Mosquito* (1911, republished with additional

---

1   Steven Sabol, *Russian Colonization of Central Asia and the Genesis of Kazak National Consciousness* (New York: Palgrave Macmillan, 2003), 95–96.

2   Ibid, 59.

3   "'Teacher of the Nation': Ahmet Baitursynov," Farabi University, accessed June 13, 2025, https://farabi.university/news/89626?lang=en.

4   Akhmet Baitursynov, *Shygharmalary: Ōleṇgder, audarmalar, zertteūler* [Collected Works: Verse, translations, investigations] (Almaty: Zhazushy, 1989), 3–4.

poems in 1922). He also wrote for the journal *Ah, Alas* (1911–1915) and, later, the more politically conscious and progressive *Kazakh* (1913–1918), where he would serve on the editorial board.[5] These publications positioned Baitursynov among the leading Kazakh writers.

After the Bolshevik Revolution began in 1917, the territories of the Russian Empire were neither tsarist nor Bolshevik. As a consequence, a group of Kazakh intellectuals founded the Alash Orda, the provisional governing body of the Alash Autonomy. This proto-state advocated for the equality of men and women, universal compulsory education, marriage age requirements for girls, and the use of Baitursynov's standardization of Kazakh grammar in the national press.[6] Seeing this proto-state as a model for a decolonized and democratic Kazakh nation, and as a natural candidate, Baitursynov joined the provisional government in 1917 and became a leader and organizer.[7]

By 1919, however, Soviet forces had effectively disrupted the Alash Orda and integrated the nation into the newly formed Soviet Union. Having defeated the Russian Empire's White Army in 1920, the Bolsheviks occupied the Alash Autonomy and renamed it the Kirgiz Autonomous Soviet Socialist Republic. Recusing himself from the provisional government in 1919, Baitursynov was granted amnesty and joined the Bolshevik Party in measured hope of a democratic future for the territory. He served on the Committee of Deputies of the Constituent Assembly, was deputy chairman of the Revolutionary Committee of the Kazakh Kraj, and became commissar of enlightenment in 1920.[8] As commissar, he reformed Kazakh education standards and helped establish the first university in the territory.

As Soviet ideology became more uniform and anti-nationalist, Baitursynov, along with many other political activists, were purged from the communist party in 1924. In 1929, Baitursynov was imprisoned for his

---

5 Martha Brill Olcott, *The Kazakhs*. Studies of Nationalities in the USSR (Stanford University, CA: Hoover Institution Press, 1987), 115.

6 Diana Amanzholova, "На изломе. Алаш в етнополитическои истории Казакхстана" [At the break: Alash in the ethnopolitical history of Kazakhstan] (Almaty: Taymas, 2011), 172.

7 Mambet Koigeldiev, "The Alash Movement and the Soviet Government: A Difference of Positions," in *Empire, Islam, and Politics in Central Eurasia*, ed. Tomohiko Uyama (Sapporo: Slavic Research Center, 2007), 160.

8 Tomohiko Uyama, "The Geography of Civilizations: A Spatial Analysis of the Kazakh Intelligentsia's Activities, from the Mid-Nineteenth to the Early Twentieth Century," in *Regions: A Prism to View the Slavic-Eurasian World: Towards a Discipline of "Regionology,"* ed. Kimitaka Matsuzato (Sapporo: Slavic Research Center, 2000), 91.

prerevolutionary political activity and was first sent to Qyzylorda, before being transferred to Arkhangelsk.[9] With the help of Ekaterina Peshkova, the wife of Russian writer Maxim Gorky, Baitursynov was released in 1934 and reunited with his family.[10] In 1937, along with many other Soviet intellectuals, writers, and artists during the Great Purge, he was sent to a gulag and executed.

Like most work of the intellectuals killed in the Great Purge, Baitursynov's writings on linguistics, education, and politics, as well as his poetry, were suppressed following his death. In 1989, along with many similar figures, he was rehabilitated as part of Mikhail Gorbachev's glasnost policy of openness and transparency, and his texts were collected and published in Kazakh in 1990. Baitursynov is today recognized as one of the intellectual forefathers of modern Kazakhstan, with *Mosquito* being his best-known work.

First published in 1911, the expanded 1922 edition of *Mosquito* consists of thirty-six poems, including some adaptations from Russian, ranging in length from six to over 150 lines.[11] Addressing a yet-to-exist Kazakh nation, *Mosquito* is Baitursynov's most overtly political manuscript. Speaking to his people, and the many future sons and daughters of the imagined nation, his intentions in the book are clear, as we see in the opening lines of the poem "Author's Note": to buzz around the sleeping Kazakh populace and wake them.

Despite his written intentions, however, the general public was unable to read *Mosquito*. According to a Soviet census, less than 4 percent of people in Central Asia were literate in 1920.[12] Due to the USSR's exceptionally strong commitment to education, Kazakhstan now has a literacy rate of 99.8 percent, one of the highest in the world.[13] In many of the poems in *Mosquito*—"To My People," "To My Kin," and "Kazakhness," for example—we can see Baitursynov's declarations to his compatriots, but in a form that

---

9 Sabol, *Russian Colonization of Central Asia*, 115.

10 Amanqos Mektepov, "Akhmet Baitursynov," in *Қызыл қырғын 37-де опат болғандар*, ed. Qaiyrzhan Qasenov and Amirkhan Torekhanov (Almaty: Taymas, 1994), 12.

11 The 1922 edition features additional poems and translations that offer insight into Baitursynov not only as the aspiring writer and educator of 1911, but also the political revolutionary and vocal critic he had become by 1922.

12 Ronald Liebowitz, "Education and Literacy Data in Russian and Soviet Censuses," in *Research Guide to the Russian and Soviet Censuses*, ed. Ralph S. Clem (Ithaca, NY: Cornell University Press, 1986), 161.

13 "Literacy Rate by Country 2025," World Population Review, accessed August 1, 2025, https://worldpopulationreview.com/country-rankings/literacy-rate-by-country.

would mostly circulate among the intelligentsia, needing to be spread orally to the illiterate population. These poems express a hope for a future that wouldn't exist until eighty years after their publication, with the formation of Kazakhstan in 1991. Judging from the large celebrations held in 2022 to mark Baitursynov's 150th anniversary,[14] the book is perhaps more relevant today than when it was first released.

Originally written in his own reformed Kazakh script, *Mosquito* is Baitursynov's attempt to create a national literature. His "new" literary Kazakh language draws upon his Islamic education, contains Arabic, Farsi, and Ottoman Turkish loan words, and only rarely includes the colonial Russian tongue, in which Baitursynov was also fluent. The poems also feature the Islamic elements of Kazakh culture, despite *Kazakh*'s secularism,[15] and arguably prefigure Kazakhstan's contemporary relation to the religion.[16]

Much like Alexander Pushkin in the early nineteenth century, Baitursynov also includes poems from non-Kazakh sources in *Mosquito* in an attempt to assert the Kazakh language's ability to bear a national literature itself. Adapting poems from Pushkin, Voltaire (as translated by Pushkin), Lermontov, Krylov, Nadson, and Zhadovskaya, Baitursynov chose fables and legends not only for their linguistic merit but for their value to his people. It is for that reason that he clearly instructs the reader on the meanings and morality of the translated fables by often adding addendums in verse to each poem. While some are set beneath individual poems as moral lessons, others make subtle connections between another poem, the struggles of the Kazakh people, and his own travails.

Thus, the book is written to the future, to Baitursynov's imagined Kazakh nation. While contemporary Kazakhstan would have certainly been unrecognizable to Baitursynov, *Mosquito* stands as a unique vision of the

---

14 Assel Satubaldina, "Upcoming Birthday Anniversaries of Kazakhstan's Ahmet Baitursynov, Roza Baglanova Included in UNESCO List of Anniversaries," *Astana Times*, November 26, 2021, https://astanatimes.com/2021/11/upcoming-birthday-anniversaries-of-kazakhstans-ahmet-baitursynov-roza-baglanova-included-in-unesco-list-of-anniversaries/.

15 Diana T. Kudaibergenova, *Rewriting the Nation in Modern Kazakh Literature: Elites and Narratives* (Lanham, MD: Lexington Books, 2017), 5.

16 All religious groups must be registered with the Kazakhstan government and are closely supervised by governing bodies. In this attempt to quell radicalism and proselytism, however, religious freedom in Kazakhstan is greatly undermined as described by "Freedom in the World 2023: Kazakhstan," Freedom House, https://freedomhouse.org/country/kazakhstan/freedom-world/2023.

Kazakh past, present, and future. He calls for changes in culture, traditions, education, and more in a Kazakh script and a Kazakh literature addressed to a Kazakh people. Baitursynov's vision for his compatriots is flawed, as all singular visions are, but it always supports a Kazakh nation governed by Kazakhs. It's a vision as clear, critical, and demanding as could be. It's *Mosquito*.

Translator's Note

When I decided to translate Akhmet Baitursynov's poems, I had no idea what I was getting into. I knew he was a member of the Alash Orda and I knew he adapted the Kazakh script, but I didn't fully understand his poems until I'd actually translated them. That might sound odd coming from a translator of his work, but reading and translating Baitursynov's poetry was, for me, a slow and thoughtful process.

I first encountered the Kazakh language as a Peace Corps Volunteer living in Mongolia's westernmost province of Bayan-Ölgiĭ. There, the ethnic minority of Kazakhs in the country made up the vast majority of the province. I learned to speak Kazakh with a Mongolian dialect, "Ölgiĭshe" as local friends would joke, roughly meaning "Ölgiĭ-speak," that they assured me would sound parochial to Kazakh speakers in Kazakhstan. After spending a summer in what was then Astana and beginning formal study of the language, and continuing that formal study throughout my master's program in Russian, Eastern European and Eurasian studies at Stanford University, and another summer at the University of Wisconsin-Madison's CESSI program, I began to remedy my shortcomings. I was firmly rooted in the Kazakh language—or so I thought.

Translating Kazakh poses the same difficulties as translating many Turkic languages in that Kazakh syntax follows a subject, object, verb sentence structure. While this may seem like a simple rearrangement, it changes the order in which information is relayed to us, something especially important in poetry. If I were to maintain that ordering throughout, to an English-speaking audience, sound like Yoda in *The Empire Strikes Back*, Baitursynov might. I've attempted to preserve the word order as much as possible, but there are many instances in which it would sound too hollow to the English-reading ear; in such cases, I switched to a subject, verb, object sequence. This can be seen in the fifth line of the second poem of the collection, "Author's Note":

Үстінде	ұйықтағанның	айнала	ұшып
Above	(person) sleeping	around	flying

A literal translation might read:

Above the sleeping person around it flew

However, the word order doesn't sound quite right. My own translation reads:

Circling above them

This line very much follows standard English syntax with its subject, verb, object construction. While "around" is omitted, "circling" implies the meaning of the line while also conveying the irritating position of the mosquito. In "Author's Note," I've also translated "mosquito" as "enemy" in the first line to indicate the low estimation of the mosquito in Kazakh culture. "Qarlyghashtyng qŭĭryghy nege aĭyr" (Why the swallow's tail is forked) is not only a popular Kazakh folk tale and the subject and title of the first Kazakh animated film (1967), but hinges on the oppositional nature of the mosquito.[17] As this is an "Author's Note" and the main thematic poem in the collection, the choice of the mosquito gives the reader a sense of the rhetoric Baitursynov will use throughout *Mosquito*. He'll not only be a champion of the Kazakh people, but also an irritating opponent to the ways in which newly sedentary Kazakh life, as he saw it, was insufficient for a thriving nation.

Given that in Baitursynov's poems verbs often, but not always, occupy the last word of the poetic line, rhyming was easily achieved through the final syllables of the varying verbs. As English is not an agglutinative language and does not compound endings, which roughly replaces the need for prepositions, there is simply no way to attempt a rhyme. Baitursynov's ease with rhyme is impossible to replicate in English, then, and I have only attempted to do so in a few instances. Instead of rhyme, I chose to focus on musicality and resonance.

Another interesting aspect Baitursynov's poetry poses for the translator is his liberal use of "intentional future" tenses. Where English speakers say "will" in the majority of our future tenses, implying a natural control of the future, Kazakh uses multiple tenses ranging from "could" to "probably will" to "most likely will" to "will." While English certainly has the ability to express

---

17 Jake Zawlacki, "The Allegorical Aĭdahar: An Animated Look at Kazakh National Identity," *FOLKLORICA—Journal of the Slavic, East European, and Eurasian Folklore Association* 23 (2019): 43–76.

these possible futures, they are much more common in Kazakh. This is best seen in the first two lines of "A Writer's Joy."

Бұл	сөзді	біреу	алмас,	біреу	алар,
This	Word	One of	Not take,	One of	Take,
			(Future conditional)		(Future intentional)
			"I might not take"		"I probably will take"

Құлағын	біреу	салмас,	біреу	салар.
An ear	One of	Not warn,	One of	Warn.
		(Future conditional)		(Future intentional)
		"I might not warn"		"I probably will warn"

To translate the conditional futures and intentional futures literally would sound remarkably clunky in English. It would require multiple words to capture what Baitursynov means when he employs simple verb endings *-ar* or *-as*. Instead, I often let the language make its own suggestion of meanings. My translation reads:

> A word alone I might not take, I might,
> An ear alone I might not warn, I might.

Here, "might" is closest to retaining the meaning and possibility that is so easily stated in the Kazakh. While the shift in degrees from the conditional to the intentional is lost in the translation, the meaning in that last "I probably will take" or "I probably will warn" is shortened to "I might" in the hope of keeping some of that original repetition of endings. Also, by chance, this shortening plays on the double meaning of "might" (strength or power), building on the possibility, and power, of Baitursynov's words as described in the poem.

Kazakh also poses a unique challenge in its lack of articles. It's therefore up to the reader to determine the context of nouns in Kazakh as either "a" or "the." This is best demonstrated in the first three lines of the third stanza of "Pieces, Gathered."

Қарқылдар	қарға,
Caw	Crow,
(Future intentional)	

Шиқылдар   арба,
Creak, squeak   Cart,
(Future intentional)

Бой   сүйсінер   сазы   жоқ.
Body   Be admired   Melody   No.
               (Future intentional)

While "Crow might caw" and "Cart might creak" are certainly possible, they wouldn't convey the implied article Baitursynov intends as I understand him. I've translated these three lines as,

> The crow will caw,
> The cart will creak,
>> But a rhythm won't be felt.

In choosing "the" over "a," I hope to use the different degrees of specificity to build towards the final line of the sentence. Switching from "the crow" and "the cart" to "a rhythm" implies the certainty of subjects and their actions in the first two lines, and the impossibility of admiration in the last. Whenever using articles, I tried to find markers within the lines that would determine the best fit.

There were also difficulties in translating work from an early period of Kazakh written literature. In contemporary Kazakh, "literary" Kazakh is referred to as "ädebi" and maintains a qualitative difference from spoken Kazakh. While many Kazakh people are fluent in speech, their reading ability varies because of changes in the written form of the language. Not only do some verbal forms change from written to spoken, but sentence structure—especially in poetry—can flex beyond the regularly structured syntax of Kazakh. This is further complicated by early Kazakh writers' wish to establish a written language, which often resulted in borrowing words from other languages.

It's here that we see Baitursynov's traditional training in Arabic, Farsi, and Turkish find its way into his work, and subsequently, the incredibly small, but growing, body of written Kazakh literature at the time. If the first hurdle is the nuanced complexity of "literary" written Kazakh today, then the second comes in translating the earliest forms of that type of Kazakh literature. Baitursynov's use of what would now be considered archaic terms, spellings that have since evolved, and words from other languages can make parsing a word or tense more challenging.

Things become even more difficult when we understand Baitursynov to be experimenting with the written Kazakh poetic line. His poems often combine the literal and abstract, introduce new grammar into the language, and can switch from impressionistic to didactic in just a few words. Maximizing the agglutinative grammar of Kazakh, Baitursynov not only confronted the Kazakh people in his political poems, but stretched the very limits of what written Kazakh could be. Baitursynov and his editors even offered footnotes in the 1922 version to help native Kazakh speakers become familiar with his terms. (My English footnotes attempt to clarify culturally specific terms that have no direct English analog.)

It is for these reasons that I decided to privilege what I understand to be the essence of Baitursynov's poetry, focusing on lines rather than a literal, word-for-word translation. In rendering the poems as individual poetic lines instead of full sentences—which may span several lines—my goal was to preserve the order in which Baitursynov presents images, emotions, and ideas to the reader. While at times the construction of a sentence or poem may feel peculiar to an English reader, it's what Baitursynov intended to a Kazakh audience. It is also my hope to capture his turn of the century experimental style and preserve the written Kazakh language that was just beginning to take shape. For that reason, many contemporary Kazakh readers may also find his diction, spelling, phrasing, line construction, indentations, and decorations unusual. To illustrate just how different the written language of Baitursynov was, a selection of his articles for *Kazakh* was republished as part of a celebration marking Baitursynov's 150th birthday, substantially updated with modern vocabulary, spellings, and grammar so contemporary Kazakh readers could understand him, despite being written in the same language. It is my hope to have reproduced his voice throughout this process, allowing him to admonish, praise, question, and ponder with as little interference as possible. Ultimately, the goal of this translation is to introduce the work of Akhmet Baitursynov to English-language readers, and I hope my version of *Mosquito* becomes one of many, with new translators improving upon the imperfect work before them.

I would also like to say how incredibly grateful I am to the many people who have helped me in this task. While working on *Mosquito*, my first foray into literary translation, I quickly realized that translation is a much less solitary act than the other forms of writing I've done, and I simply couldn't have finished this work alone. Translating Baitursynov meant texting Sophia Syltanqan, my Kazakh sister in Mongolia, in the wee hours of my night and in her morning to parse a troubling line. If she didn't understand it, she would discuss it with the Kazakh-language teachers at Ölgiĭ Fourth School before sending me their collective thoughts. Translating also meant working very closely with Symbat Nartay, a world literature student at Nazarbayev University, who double-checked that I hadn't missed idioms, phrasal verbs, or unfamiliar vocabulary, and helped me think through particularly difficult lines. I'm grateful for both her devotion to the material and her friendship. I also met weekly with Ariel Francisco, assistant professor at Louisiana State University and renowned translator, at French Truck in Baton Rouge, Louisiana, to then fine-tune the English version. It meant gaining the confidence, through the support of Sophia, Symbat, and Ariel, to push beyond the literal meaning of the words and capture what Baitursynov is saying in his lines.

If I've developed a philosophy of translation, it's that it is a creative, communal, and imperfect act. There is no 1:1 English analog to the original Kazakh. While it's impossible to reproduce Baitursynov's rhyming patterns, grammatical intricacies, and experimental nuances, with the help of many, I've done my very best to bring *Mosquito* to the English-speaking world. If there are any failures or shortcomings in my translations, they are mine and mine alone. If there are any successes or lines that hit you just right, they're the shared successes of those who have aided in this project. But most of all, they're Akhmet's.

References

Amanzholova, Diana. "На изломе. Алаш в етнополитическои истории Казакхстана" [At the Break. Alash in the Ethnopolitical History of Kazakhstan]. Almaty: Taymas, 2011.

Baitursynov, Akhmet. *Shygharmalary: Öleṅgder, audarmalar, zertteüler* [Collected Works: Verse, translations, investigations]. Almaty: Zhazushy, 1989.

"'Teacher of the Nation': Ahmet Baitursynov." Farabi University. Accessed June 13, 2025. https://farabi.university/news/89626?lang=en.

Koigeldiev, Mambet. "The Alash Movement and the Soviet Government: A Difference of Positions." In *Empire, Islam, and Politics in Central Eurasia*, edited by Tomohiko Uyama, 153–184. Sapporo: Slavic Research Center, 2007.

Kudaibergenova, Diana T. *Rewriting the Nation in Modern Kazakh Literature : Elites and Narratives*. Lanham, MD: Lexington Books, 2017.

Liebowitz, Ronald. "Education and Literacy Data in Russian and Soviet Censuses." In *Research Guide to the Russian and Soviet Censuses*, edited by Ralph S. Clem, 155–170. Ithaca, NY: Cornell University Press, 1986.

Mektepov, Amanqos. "Akhmet Baitursynov." In *Қызыл қырғын 37-де опат болғандар*. Edited by Qaiyrzhan Qasenov and Amirkhan Torekhanov, 9–12. Almaty: Taymas, 1994.

Olcott, Martha Brill. *The Kazakhs. Studies of Nationalities in the USSR*. Stanford, CA: Hoover Institution Press, 1987.

Sabol, Steven. *Russian Colonization of Central Asia and the Genesis of Kazak National Consciousness*. New York: Palgrave Macmillan, 2003.

Satubaldina, Assel. "Upcoming Birthday Anniversaries of Kazakhstan's Ahmet Baitursynuov, Roza Baglanova Included in UNESCO List of Anniversaries." *Astana Times*. November 26, 2021. https://astanatimes.com/2021/11/upcoming-birthday-anniversaries-of-kazakhstans-ahmet-baitursynov-roza-baglanova-included-in-unesco-list-of-anniversaries/.

Uyama, Tomohiko. "The Geography of Civilizations: A Spatial Analysis of the Kazakh Intelligentsia's Activities, from the Mid-Nineteenth to the Early Twentieth Century." In *Regions: A Prism to View the Slavic-Eurasian World: Towards a Discipline of "Regionology,"* edited by Kimitaka Matsuzato, 70–99. Sapporo: Slavic Research Center, 2000.

"Literacy Rate by Country 2025." World Population Review. Accessed August 1, 2025. https://worldpopulationreview.com/country-rankings/literacy-rate-by-country.

Zawlacki, Jake. "The Allegorical Aïdahar: An Animated Look at Kazakh National Identity." *FOLKLORICA—Journal of the Slavic, East European, and Eurasian Folklore Association* 23 (2019): 43–76.

Маса

Түсіне қараб,
Ішінен түңілме!
Күшіне қараб,
Ісінен түңілме.

Mosquito

Seeing dreams,
Hope from within!
Seeing strength,
Hope from our work.

Сөз Иесінен

Ызыңдаб ұшқан мынау біздің маса:
Саб-сары, айақтары ұзын маса;
Өзіне біткен түсі өзгерілмес
Дегенмен қара йаки қызыл маса.

Үстінде ұйықтағанның айнала ұшыб,
Қаққы жеб, қанаттары бұзылғанша,
Ұйқысын аз да болса бөлмес пе екен,
Қоймастан құлағына ызыңдаса?!

Author's Note

Our enemy buzzes around:
Yellow, long-legged mosquito;
Its natural color unchanged,
Both black, even red mosquito.

Circling above them,
Mocking, flying till wings break.
Maybe one will awaken—
That relentless buzzing in our ear?

Жазушының Қанағаты

Бұл сөзді біреу алмас, біреу алар,
Құлағын біреу салмас, біреу салар.
Теб-тегіс көбке ұнау оңай емес,
Кейіне жарамаса, кейіне жарар.

Қайсысы ықыласын салыб тыңдаб,
Жаратбай қайсыбірі, теріс қарар.
Дүниаде сүйгенім бар, күйгенім бар
Солардан аз да болса белгі қалар.

~~~~~~~~~~
~~~~~~~~~~

A Writer's Joy

A word alone I might not take, I might,
An ear alone I might not warn, I might.
Simplicity is not simple,
Maybe words didn't fit, maybe they did.

To which purpose will I arrive,
Not just another, maybe failure.
In this world I have my love, my passion—
Although small, I'll leave my mark.

~~~~~~~~~~
~~~~~~~~~~

Туысыма

Болармын нағыб риза тұуысыма?
Тұуыббын таршылықдың ұуысында.
Шамам жоқ, жан жағыма қол созарлық,
Тар көрдің тығылғандай қуысына.

Айта алмай шын сөзіңді қорғалайсын,
Тұуғаның бүйтіб хор боб құрысын да!
Бар пайдаң өз басыңнан артылмаса,
Мал ғұрлы мағына жоқ тұрысыңда.

~~~~~~~~~~
~~~~~~~~~~

To My Kin

Why should I be satisfied with you?
I was born with empty hands.
Unable to reach out,
Groping in the grave's abyss.

You can't speak truth, but defend,
Kin like you can leave us!
Talent wasted only on yourself,
Just another meaningless animal.

~~~~~~~~~~
~~~~~~~~~~

Жадовскайадан

Мінсіз таса меруерд
    Сұу түбінде жатады;
Мінсіз таза асыл сөз
    Ой түбінде жатады;
Сұу түбінде жатқан зат,
    Жел толқытса шығады,
Ой түбінде жатқан сөз
    Шер толықытса шығады.

From Zhadovskaya[*]

Flawless pearl
    Lying beneath the water;
Precious word
    Lying beneath a thought;
An object beneath the water
    A storm may stir.
A word beneath a thought
    A heavy heart may lighten.

---

[*] Adapted to the Kazakh from Yulia Zhadovskaya's Russian version, "Лучший перл таится…" (1843).

Хожа Насретдин Ақылы

Бір күні Хожа Насретдин жиылған жұртқа үгіт ай-туға мінбеге шығыб: «Азаматтар! Мен сөйлейін деб тұрғаным ненің жайы, білесіңдер ме?» дебді. Жұрт: «Жоқ білмейміз!» дебді. Хожа: «Білмесеңдер білмейтін нәрселеріңді мен қалай сөйлеймін» деб мінбеден түсібді. Жұрт қамтама қалыб, білмейміз дегеніміз ағат болған екен, енді сұраса білмесек те білеміз деб айталық дебді.

Екінші рет Хожа мінбеге шығыб тағы сұрабды:

«Азаматтар! Мен не жайын сөйлемекпін, білесіңдер ме?» деб. «Білеміз! Білеміз!» деб жұртдың бәрі шұулабды. «Өздерің біліб тұрсаңдар, мен несін айтайын» деб Хожа мінбеден тағы түсібді. Жиылған адамдар, айтады: «енді сұраса білетіндер де, білмейтіндер де бар» деб айтбақшы болыб, сөз айтысды.

Үшінші рет Хожа мінбеге шығыб бұрынғыдай тағы сұрағанда, жиылғандар «білетініміз де бар, білмейтініміз де бар» дебді. «Олай болса, білетіндерің білмейтіндеріңді үйретсін, білмейтіндерің білетіндеріңнен үйренсін!» деб Хожа мінбеден түсібді де жүріб кетібді.

~~~~~~~~~~
~~~~~~~~~~

Khoja Nasreddin's Cunning

One day Khoja Nasreddin gathered the people and lectured from a platform. "Citizens! Do you know what I'll speak to you about?" he said.

"No, we don't know!" said the crowd.

"Those who don't know won't know about the things I'll talk about," Khoja said coming down from the platform.

The people spoke to each other, saying, "They were wrong to say they didn't know. If he asks again we'll say we know even if we don't."

The second time Khoja stood on the platform he asked, "Citizens! What I'm talking about, do you know?"

"We know! We know!" said all of the people.

"Then you yourselves already know what I'll say," said Khoja coming down from the platform once more.

The crowd whispered to each other. "Now, if he asks, say some know and some don't," they promised.

The third time Khoja stood on the platform and asked again, the crowd said, "There are some who know, and some who don't."

"If that's so, then have those who know teach those who don't, and those who don't learn from those who do!" said Khoja as he set off.

~~~~~~~~~~
~~~~~~~~~~

Оқұуға Шақырұу

Балалар! Оқуға бар! Жатба қараб!
Жуыныб, киініндер шабшаң-рақ!
Шақырды тауық мана әлдеқашан;
Қараб тұр терезеден күн жылтыраб.

Адам да, ұшқан құс да, жүрген аң да,
Жұмыссыз тек тұрған жоқ ешбір жан да:
Кішкене қоңыз да жүр, жүгін сүйреб,
Барады аралар да ұшыб балға.

Күн ашық, тоғайлар шад, ың-жың орман,
Ойаныб жан-мақұлық түнде қонған;
Шығады тоқылдақдың тоқ-тоқ даусы;
Сайрағы сарғалдақдың сыңғырлаған.

Өзенде балықшылар ау қараб жүр;
Тоғайда орақ даусы шаң-шұң орған.
Аллалаб, ал кітабды қолдарыңа!
Құлдарын Құдай сүймес жалқау болған.

~~~~~~~~~~
~~~~~~~~~~

Invitation to Study

Children! Go study! Don't be lazy!
Wash up, get dressed, come quick!
Just now the rooster called us;
Sunshine peeks through the window.

Humans, flying birds, roaming beasts,
Not one without work:
Little bugs walk, carrying their loads,
The bees flying to honey.

An open sun, playful trees, a forest hum,
Everything waking from the night;
Woodpeckers pecking;
Singing buttercups ringing.

Fishermen search the river;
Sickles sound the forest.
For Allah, read your books!
Lazy servants of God may not be loved.

~~~~~~~~~~~
~~~~~~~~~~~

Нәбек Аты

Арабдың Нәбек жалғыз аты; –
Сол екен болған малы, мүлкі, заты,
Озбайтын шабса жылқы асқан жүйрік,
Бітбеген өзге атдарға түр сифаты.

Күн сайын жал құирығын сүзіб тараб;
Сұуарыб мезгілімен, жемдеб қараб
Өткізбей күндіз ыстық, түнде суық
Адамнан атын артық күтеді араб.

Бар екен Дайыр деген бір асқан бай
Малы көб, түрлі бұйым бәріне сай,
Мұңы зор: сонша байлық ортасында:
Аты жоқ жылқысында жарлы атындай.

Ал деді, айамады малын, затын;
Алмады, бермеді де Нәбек атын:
Атқұмар атын қимас, жанын қиар, –
Атынан еш нәрсе жоқ оған жақын.

Дайырда күндіз күлкі, түнде ұйқы жоқ;
Жарлыдай жалғыз атты, бай сйқы жоқ;
Алмаққа Нәбек атын амалменен,
Ойлайды алдайын деб бір фақыр боб.

Жүретін Нәбек һаман жолын біліб,
Үстіне сылқым-сылқым киім іліб,
Аурұу, халі мүшкіл, мүсәпірше.
Отырды жол шетінде – аһ, үһілеб.

Оңаша, жолдасы жоқ, жалғыз өзі
Нәбекті келе жатқан көрді көзі
Өтерде нақ қасынан, бишарасыб,
Ыңқылдаб, міне Дайыр айтқан сөзі:

«Е, жаным! Мен жолаушы, жолым алыс,
Адам жоқ бұл маңайда маған таныс,
Аурұу, дәм татбаған үш күндей аш,
Орынымнан жылжу маған қиын жұмыс.
Атыңмен анау елдің ортасына,
Жеткізсең берер едім көб-көб алғыс!»

Тоқтатыб, басын тартыб, Нәбек атды
«Жарайды, мінгесе ғой, кел!» деб айтды.
Сөйлейді тағы Дайыр, жыламсыраб:
«Халім жоқ, міне алмаймын, дертім қатты.»

Атынан бұл сөзді естіб, түсті Нәбек
Көтеріб мінгізді ерге сүйеб, демеб.
Тиүуі тізгін қолға мұң-ақ екен
Жөнелді, бір тебініб, Дәкең шүу деб.

Шығыр аб оқ бойы жер, қараб кейін,
Ойлайды: бірдеме оған деб кетейін.
«Әй, Нәбек! Кім екенім білдің бе енді?
Атыңмен қоштас, аңқау, сорлы ақбейіл!»

«Тұра тұр! Нәбек айтды, тоқтаб солай,
Атыма асық еді адам талай.
Тілейтін жалғыз сенен тілегім сол –
Адамға айта көрме алдың қалай!»

«Бұ не сөз? Не тілек!» деб бай таңданды,
Мәнісін білейінші деб ойланды:
«Айтба деб, сонша өтініб, жалынасың,
Көрерсің айтсам онан не залалды?»

«Ойлама!» Нәбек айтды «арбайды деб;
Қол жетбей, тілін құраб, жалғайды деб;
Оқиға бұл секілді шықса аузыңнан,
Білгейсің! Жайылмай, жай қалмайды деб.
Қалайша алғаныңды жұрт естісе,
Қарасбас шын фақырға алдайды деб.»

Мұны естіб, Дайыр жылдам атдан түсді:
Ұққанға адал сөзден бар ма күшті?
Құлашын жайыб, қойнын ашыб келіб,
Нәбекті сүйіб Дайыр, мойнын құшды.

~~~~~~~~~~

Ебі көб, дорбасы жоқ қайыршылар,
Ебіне Хұдай көнсе, байып шығар!
Арымай алдырғанға Нәбекшілеб,
Адам аз айтқанды ұғыб Дайыршылар.

Жақын бол, жақындықды ебім дейді,
Бергенді алдым еббен тегін дейді.
Қайтармай, қарыз алыб қайбіреулер
Алдадым, бермей кеттім, жедім дейді.

Осындай ер басына іс көб келер!
Білмесбіз: кімге қалай, кім дөб келер!
Сұмдығы сұраушының азаймаса.
Не жөн бар? Қайырсыз деб жұртқа өкпелер!
~~~~~~~~~~

Năbek's Horse

An Arab named Năbek had a single horse;
An animal, an asset, an object,
There wasn't a horse faster,
To all others unparalleled.

Every day combing its mane and tail;
Giving water, feeding, watching
In daytime heat and freezing nights
The Arab cared for the horse better than a person.

There was also Daĭyr, a rich man,
With a large flock, many kinds of jewelry,
But deeply sad despite his wealth:
He had no horse, like a pauper.

"Take whatever, my animals, my things";
But Năbek didn't take, not trading his horse:
The horse-lover unwilling, would rather give his soul,
Nothing closer to him than his horse.

Daĭyr couldn't laugh at day, nor sleep at night;
Lower than a poor man's single horse, the rich man had none;

He might take Năbek's horse with a plan,
Thinking to deceive him dressed as a fakir.[*]

Knowing where Năbek would gallop,
Wearing his stylish clothes,
Ill, destitute, and homeless,
He sat along a road and sighed.

Alone, no companion, just himself,
He saw Năbek arriving,
Passing close, and provoked pity,
Groaning, Daĭyr said this:

"Oh, my soul! I'm a traveler, my journey long,
No one around here knows me,
I'm sick, gone hungry for three days,
Hard for me to move from this place.
Help me with your horse to the central region,
I'll be forever grateful if you give it to me!"

Stopping, Năbek pulling his horse to the side,
"Alright, if you want to ride, come!" he said.
Near tears, Daĭyr spoke:
"I'm powerless, I can't mount it, my illness too strong."

After hearing these words, Năbek dismounted,
Helping him upon the horse with care.
But as soon as he grabbed the reins
He bolted with a kick, Daĭyr yelling, "Shoo!"

He rode as fast as a shot, then looked back,
Thinking: I should say something before leaving.
"Hey, Năbek! Do you recognize me now?
Say goodbye to your horse, naive, bleeding heart!"

---

[*]   Islamic term for Sufi Muslim ascetics.

"Wait!" Năbek said, "Just wait.
Many drawn to my horse.
Praying for this single wish—
Don't tell anyone how you got it!"

"What are these words? What wish!" asked Daĭyr surprised,
Thinking through their meaning:
"You're asking me not to tell that I begged,
What harm could this cause?"

"Don't think I'm deceiving you," said Năbek,
"My hand can't reach the horse, my tongue couldn't either;
If a story like this comes from your mouth,
You should know this! It will spread around.
If people heard how you took my horse,
They'll think all fakirs will deceive them."

Hearing this, Daĭyr quickly dismounted;
Is there something stronger than truth to the understanding?
Raising both hands, coming openly,
Daĭyr kissed Năbek and hugged him.

~~~~~~~~~~~

Able-bodied, no belongings for beggars,
If God agreed, they would be wealthy!
Few would remain strong like Năbek,
Few would understand like Daĭyr.

They call it love, generosity,
They call it a skill to take things for free.
Some people not paying their debt,
"I deceived them," "I took," "I profited," they say.

There are many tests to come!
We won't know: how and to whom, or who will pass!
If ill intentions from beggars don't stop.
Then for what? They'll be offended by lack.
~~~~~~~~~~~

Сорлы болған Мұжық

Болған соң кәсібі ұрлық ұры залым,
Ұрлауға ұйат дей ме жұртдың малын?
Ойы арам қаны қара ол неғылсын!
Біреуді зар жылатбақ, зор обалын!

Хұдай да, Құран да оған жалғыз қарын.
Сол үшін қара жерге көмген арын.
Ұры еніб бір Мұжықдың сарайына.
Сыпырыб кетіді ұрлаб қоймай бәрін.

Мұжығым жатарда бай, тұрса сорлы.
Байлықдың құр тып-типыл қалған орны.
Аһылаб, үһілейді, ұрлы алған соң,
Терімен маңдайының жеған қорды.
Туысқан, көрші, құда-құрмаласын,
Дос-жаран жиыб, Мұжық жәрдем сұрады

«Қайғымды,» Мұжық айтды, «шағам, жұртым!
Сендерден жақын кімді табам, жұртым!
Ұшыраб зор қазаға, жайым мынау!
Не көмек бересіндер маған, жұртым?»

Жиылыб келген өңшең жақындары,
Мұжыққа ақыл айтыб жатыр бәрі
Сорлыға бар мүлкінен жұрдай болған
Мінеки берген көмек-ақылдары:

Карп деген бөлесі айтды: «Әуел басда
Бай деб ат керек еді шығармасқа!»
Құдасы Клим айтды: «Мұнан бұлай
Сарайды үйден оқшау салдырмасқа!»

Айтады көрші мұжық бір жасырақ:
«Болғаннан емес қой бұл сарай жырақ;
Қабаған кісі алатын төбеттерден
Қораға қоймағаннан ит асыраб.

Қаншығым балалады күні кеше,
Ал, сонан, айамайын керегінше!

Бірталай, үйшік толған күшігі бар,
Ішінен табылатын қандай десе.
Көршіме көңілі жарым қимаймын ба?
Обалын мойныма артыб, өлтіргенше!»

Жүз ақыл берген шығар келген бәрі;
Бірі олай, бірі бұлай деб жас, кәрі.
Айамай тіл көмегін беріб, беріб,
Бір адам қарасбады сөзден әрі.

Ей, Мұжық! Жұртқа сенбе өзіңе сен!
Өледі аштан қонақ әрі-сәрі.
«Ауызыңды құрғақ қасық босқа қажар»
Шығынға құр айтқан сөз болмас дәрі.

~~~~~~~~~~

Бұл сөздің мағынасы емес терең,
Сонда да қорытуын айтыб берем;
Һәр түрлі сыналатын жер болмаса,
Достықты, жақындықты шын-ақ дер ем;
Жаб жақын жайшылықда көб дос жарды,
Мен неге жамандықда сирек көрем?

Тар кезең, талма жерде табылу жоқ;
Қалады құлақдары болыб керең.
Осындай дүнианың ісін байқаб,
Достық бен жақындыққа талғаб сенем.
~~~~~~~~~~

The Unlucky Peasant[*]

A thief's evil trade of cunning,
Is it a shame to steal the people's wealth?
Thoughts dirty, black blood, what do they care!
Forcing tears in others, a monstrous sin!

His God, Quran, his belly alone.
His conscience buried in darkness.
The thief entered the peasant's barn,
Swiping and stealing everything.

A peasant rich before sleep, awoke poor.
Fortune's place now empty.
Ahhhs, Ooohs, after the thief stole
Things he gathered with the sweat of his brow.
Relatives, neighbors, uncles[**] surrounding him,
Gathered with friends, the peasant asked for help.

"Misery," said the peasant, "I'll share with you!
Who's closer, my good people!
A loss befallen, this is my lot!
What help can you give?"

Gathered together, only the closest
Gave the peasant advice,
He who lost everything he had,
Words of wisdom like this:

---

[*]   Adapted to the Kazakh from Ivan Krylov's Russian version, "Крестьянин в беде" (1811).
[**]   The male relatives of each family who help in arranging a marriage.

Cousin Karp shared: "From the beginning
You shouldn't have shown your wealth!"
The father-in-law Klim, "From now on
The barn shouldn't be so far from the house!"

A neighbor spoke to the younger peasant,
"It's not because the barn is far;
You didn't take these guard dogs
To protect your livestock and barn.

The dog's litter that night,
Take as many as you need!

Lots of puppies in the hovel,
You can find whichever you want.
Wouldn't I give everything to my poor neighbor?
Better than the guilt of killing them!"

A hundred pieces of advice were given;
One this, one that, from young and old.
Everyone giving help, in words, giving,
But nothing further than speech.

Hey, peasant! Trust no one! Only yourself!
Your guests die from hunger,
"A dry spoon will torment your mouth."
Empty words aren't the cure for your loss.

~~~~~~~~~~~

Despite shallow words,
I'll summarize them;
If there are no types of tests,
Friendship, love, I'd say are true;
Closest friends stay close at ease,
But where do they go in hardship?
~~~~~~~~~~~

In that difficult time, I couldn't find joy;
Their ears turned deaf.
As such, I've seen how the world works,
I'm picky in friendship and love.

Қаздар

~~~~~~~~~~

Бір ұзын алыб қолға мықты шыбық
Қаздарын қалаға айдаб шықды мұжық.
Қуалаб байғұсдарды, келеді ұрыб,
Асығыб базар күнге жаны шығыб.

Тексерсек мұжық ісін байқаб, ойлаб,
Оған да дұрыс емес кінә қоймақ:
Асықды базар күнге, пайда көб деб,
Қаздарды ұрды ма ол босқа ойнаб?

Десеңдер: олсыз базар тарамайды
Дер едім, мұжық ісі жарамайды.
Пайдасы, базар өтіб, кетер жерде,
Қаз түгіл адамға да қарамайды.

Біздерше қаздар, бірақ, сынамады,
Оларға мұжық ісі ұнамады.
Жолыққан жолаушыға бәрі шұулаб,
Мұжықтың ісін айтыб, кінәлады.

«Бар ма екен? Бізден сірә соры қалың!
Қожасыб, қуалайды мұжық жарым.
Қорлайды ұрыб, соғыб ойламайды,
Мойнында қандай міндет қарыз барын!

Ойласа қайдан біздің асылымыз?
Румды құтқарған қаз нәсіліміз!
Айт істеб атамыздың құрметіне,
Өтбейді һәман онда жыл мейрамсыз!
Тайақ жеб жай қаздарша, жүргеніміз,
Наданға душар болыб бір білімсіз!»
~~~~~~~~~~

Қаздарға жолаушы айтды: «Тоқтаңдаршы!
Ауысқан ақыны айтыб жоқтаңдаршы!
Сендерді қадірлеуге не үшін міндет?
Мұжықды айыбты ғып боқтаңдаршы!»

«– Істеген атамыздың ісі қайда!?
Румды құтқарғаны азғантай ма?»
«Қойа тұр» жолаушы айтды, «көрдегінді!
Өздерің келтірдіңдер қанша пайда!?»

«– Айтдық ғой атамыздың еткен ісін!
Әлде өзің сөзімізге сенбеймісің?»
«– Сенемін һәм білемін атаң жайын!
Сендерді қадірлеуге деймін не үшін?
Өткізді өз бастарың қандай еңбек?
Атаңда көрде жатқан жоқ жұмысым»

«Біздің бе? . . . (*) жоқ өткізген еңбегіміз?»
«Әже жөн сыйламаса, көнбегіңіз:
Мені де атам жақсы, қадірле деб,
Таласыб қиын болар жеңбегіңіз.

Жақсы-ақ боб аталарын өткен шығар:
Ісіне қарай құрмет еткен шығар;
Қалдырмай асылынан артдағыға,
Өзімен жақсылығы кеткен шығар.

Көрдегі көмек болмас бабаларың,
Кем болса өздеріңнің бағаларың;
Көніңдер, ұрса, соқса, сойса дағы!
Болған соң қуырдақдық шамаларың».

~~~~~~~~~~

---

*   . . . Ойланыб, ойланыб.
~~~~~~~~~~

Кетермін байандасам алысқа бек:
Лайық һәр нәрсеге керек ғой еб.
Жайынан жат қаздардың сөйлеген сөз
Көбіне жақын қаздың тиетін дөб.

Бетіне көрдегінің көнін ұстаб,
Деб жүрген көріктімін қазақтар көб.
Қысқартыб сөз айағын тоқтатамын,
Солардың өкпесіне қалармын деб.

Geese[*]

———————————————

~~~~~~~~~~~

With a long strong stick,
A peasant drove the geese to the city.
Pushing the poor creatures, beating,
He hurried them to the market that day.

The pensive peasant observed, thought,
Wondered if his guilt be untrue:
To the day market, hoping for lots of profit,
Did he hit the geese in vain?

If you say the bazaar will not close without him,
I'd say the peasant's not right for this.
For his profit, crossing through the bazaar, going,
He'd hit a man like a goose, if needed.

The geese, however, never considered;
They didn't like what he did.
Seeing a passerby they all made noise,
And accused the peasant's deed.

"Is there one who's suffered this way?
Feeling his power, the stupid peasant ran after us.
Demeaning, thoughtless beating,
Not thinking how he owed such a debt!

———————————————————————————————————

[*]   Adapted to the Kazakh from Ivan Krylov's Russian version, "Гуси" (1811).
~~~~~~~~~~~

Does he know our worth?
We are the ones who protected the Romans!*
They celebrated us with a feast,
Not a year passes without being honored!
Getting hit as ordinary geese, us going,
Because we ran into a dumb peasant!"

The passerby said this:
"That's enough!
Cry about your changed state!
Why do you deserve respect?
Blame the peasant and curse him!"

"—Where is the work of our grandfathers?
Is it not enough they saved the Romans?"
"Wait," the passerby said, "Look!
What have you yourself done?"

"—We already told of our ancestors work!
Or did you not believe our words?"
"—I believed and I know your grandfather's story!
I ask why I have to respect you?
What deeds have you done yourself?
I don't care about the work of your ancestors."

"Us? . . .** We haven't done anything?"
"If you're disrespected like that, agree:
If my grandfather is good, then respect me too,
Hard for you to win the argument.

---

* During a covert attack by the Gauls in the fourth century BCE, geese alerted the Romans
to the invasion and saved the capital.
** Baitursynov writes ". . . Thinking, thinking" in the original footnote to describe the pur-
pose of the ellipsis for readers who may be unfamiliar with the grammar in what could be
its first grammatical use in the Kazakh language.

Maybe your elders passed as good long ago:
Maybe honored and respected for their deeds;
Not leaving their value for their progeny,
Maybe their good passed with them.

Your ancestors can't help you from the grave
If your own value is diminished;
Agree if you are beaten, battered, or slaughtered!
After the roast you'll see your worth."

~~~~~~~~~~~

If I'll narrate, I'll go too far:
All things need consideration.
A strange goose's words
Can change those near him.

Holding a corpse's skin to their face,
Many Kazakhs think they are beautiful.
I've summarized but I'll stop myself,
In order not to offend.
~~~~~~~~~~~

Есек пен Үкі

Үркектеу, үйір емес онша қолға,
Бір Есек ұлы сапар шықты жолға.
Есектің бойы тәуір болғанменен,
Есебде қосылмайды есі молға.

Және де бұл Есектің көзі соқыр,
Басшысыз, соқыр қалай жүрсің оңға?
Ылағыб тура жолдан, қаңғыб кетді,
Қисайыб, қыңыржақтаб шығыб жонға.

Ішіне қалың орман барыб кірд,
Білмейдін, не жол тауыб неғыб жүрді?
Күн батыб, қас қарайған уақытда,
Есектің ылаққанын Үкі көрді.

Үкі айтды мінгіз Есек мені! деді;
Мініб аб, мен бастайын сені деді;
Жолды айтыб, жөнді сілтеб мен отрысам,
Көзіңнің һеш нәрсе емес кемі деді.

Бір ауыз сөз қайырмай, Есек көнді,
Мініб аб, Үкі отырды сілтеб жөнді.
Жерлерден адыр-бұдыр аман өтіб,
Ағаштың жиегіне жақын келді.

Жол табқан қараңғыда басшысына, –
Ден қойыб, бастағыш деб, Есек сенді.
Бір кезде таң сарғайыб – машырықдан
Ағаштың арасына сәуле енді

Үкілер күндіз соқыр, түнде көргіш,
Есекең, іс мәнісін білмей ергіш
Үкіден, таң атса да айрылмайды,
Деб ойлаб Жарықда да жөн сілтегіш.
Күн шықды, жарық болды дүниа жүзі
Үкінің бұлдырайды көрмей көзі.
Өзгеге жөн көрсетіб, бастау түгіл
Әлі бар отырарлық жай – ғана өзі.

Сонда да Есегіне сыр бермеске,
Айтатын, білгішсініб, міне сөзі:
«Ал келдік жаман жерге! Енді сақтан!
Жолама! Сол жақтағы өзенге аққан.
Бетінді оң жағыңа сала жүріб,
Аман өт! Мынау жатқан ылай қақтан»
(Ол жердің өзені де, қағы да жоқ!
Білмеймін, соқыр Үкі қайдан табқан!)

Есекді Үкі билеб, алыб қолға,
Салыбды нақ ғазазыл түскен жолға.
Пәлен деб күн ілгері неғылайық,
Түскені ондай жолға бақпа? сорма?

~~~~~~~~~~~

Бұл сөзді байандаған болмас айыб!
Һәркімнің ісіне бар сөз лайық.
Көркем сөз мұнан артық таба алмадым
Тал түсде ылаққанға жолдан тайыб.

Көб білім, көбді үйретер, болмаса да,
Не пайда? Жабыққаннан құр мұңайыб,
Соқырға көрсеткенмен, көре қоймас!
Сонда да, үміт үзіб, отырмайық.
Арланбай, адасқанды әшкерелеб,
Қойалық погоннойын жұртқа жайыб.

~~~~~~~~~~~

Болады ақылсыздың мысалы есек,
Ғылымсыз надан адам соқырға есеб.
Қалбынан есек асыб ат болмайды,
Қойса да қорасына асыл төсеб.

Алтынды айағыңа басқанменен,
Болмайды асылы азыб, балшық кесек.
Жақсыны жақсы деген, мақтау емес,
Жаманды жаман десең, болмайды есек.
Қауымынан мұсылманның шыққан жолды,
Айыбба, ғазазылдың жолы десек.

Білгішсіб кей білімсіз жол айтыб жүр,
Байқасақ, не онды жол ол айтыб жүр.
Халыққа надан адам басшы болыб
Халықдың надандығын молайтыб жүр.
Наданға надандықбен, жұрт ерген соң,
Тал түсте ылақды деб соны айтыб жүр.

~~~~~~~~~~

Жазған сөз жаным ашыб Алашыма;
Алашдың адасқан аз баласына.
Қаннан қан, еткен інім бауыр жұртым!
Қараған «Қара таудың» қаласына;

Іші лас сырты таза залымдардың
Алданыб құр сыртының тазасына.
Мәз болыб байғазы алған балаларша
Сатылыб жылтыраған танасына,

Әбілдің зиаратын аттаб өтіб
Қабылдың бата қылма моласына,
Қорыққанға қос көрініб қойдай үркіб
Тығылыб дажалдың ит ханасына,
~~~~~~~~~~

Ес кетіб, сабыр қалмай сасқалақтаб.
Қорыққаннан көзің сыймай шарасына,
Ұмытыб Хұдайды да, Құранды да,
Бас ұрма, Лат – Манат ағашына!

~~~~~~~~~~
~~~~~~~~~~

The Ass and the Owl[*]

————————————————

Frightened, introverted, and closed,
A donkey bayed at traveling the road.
Despite the ass's strong stature,
His mind doesn't work well.

And this donkey's eyes were blind.
Leaderless, blind, how could it go on?
Straying off the road, roaming
Crooked, he barely reached the plateau.

He entered the thick forest,
Not knowing which path to take.
Sun setting, night following it,
An owl saw the stray donkey.

The owl said, "Donkey! Let me ride you!"
After sitting, "I'll lead you.
I'll see the road, give directions;
Your blindness won't matter."

Without a word, the donkey agreed,
Riding on, the owl sat and directed.
From uneven places they passed well,
Coming close to tree's edges.

To the leader finding the road in darkness,
Focused, accepting, the donkey trusted.
But in the gold of morning from the East
A ray beamed through the trees.

——

[*]   Adapted to the Kazakh from Ivan Krylov's Russian version, "Филин и Осёл" (1830).

Owls being blind at day, seeing only at night,
The donkey, followed unaware,
Staying with the owl even in the sun.
Thought he'd get directions in the light.
The sun rose, light covering the world,
And the owl's clouded eyes couldn't see.
Not giving directions, not a word,
Sitting still—just himself.

He wouldn't tell the donkey his secret,
Saying, arrogantly, these words:
"We came to this bad place! Now beware!
Stay away! To the left is a rushing river.
Choose the right where the river's branches run,
Pass well! This side of puddled mud."
(There was no river, and no puddles!
I don't know where the blind owl looked!)

The owl instructed the donkey, directing
To a tumble, the path of demons,
The day passed and what could they do,
Was falling this way luck? A curse?

~~~~~~~~~~~

Telling this story is not to accuse!
Every deed can be described.
I couldn't find more beautiful words than that
For the one who strayed under the noon sun.

Knowledge, teaching, couldn't be found,
What purpose? Pointless sadness,
Showing the blind, they're unable to see!
Anyway, let's not lose hope, not sit with it.
Shameless, exposing the lost one,
Spread epaulets to the people.

~~~~~~~~~~~

Thus the donkey exemplifies the ignorant,
Uneducated growing into blindness.
A donkey cannot move from this to steed,
Even with a stable's floor covered in diamonds.

Gold being stepped on by feet,
Its value untarnished, unlike clumps of mud.
Saying good is good, is no praise,
Saying bad is bad, is not stubborn.
The road far from a Muslim village,
Is it wrong to call it the demon's path?

Posing, the clueless gave directions,
If we notice, which path he says is right.
An ignorant leader of the people
Breeds ignorance in the people.
Ignorant of ignorance, getting lost at midday,
The people follow anyway.

~~~~~~~~~~

I write with concern for my tribe,
To the few lost children of Alash.*
Blood from blood, flesh from flesh, my people!
The city in the shadows of the Black Mountains.

Cores soiled, the wicked's clean countenance,
We're deceived by their appearance.
As children satisfied with small gifts
Sold for a sparkling calf.

Walking across the father's tomb,
Don't pray for the souls of the cemetery,
Being afraid, like sheep scattering,
Hiding in the devil's kennel,

---

* Encompasses the three historical tribal and territorial divisions of Kazakhs. It was also used in 1917 as the name of the provisional government Alash Orda, of which Baitursynov was a member. The term is often used synonymously with "Kazakh."
~~~~~~~~~~

Raving, patience departed, in disarray,
In fear, eyes falling from their sockets,
Forgetting God, forgetting the Quran,
Beware the effigies of Allat* and Manat!**

~~~~~~~~~~

---

* A pre-Arabic goddess worshipped throughout the Arabian peninsula associated with war, peace, and prosperity.

** A pre-Arabic goddess worshipped throughout the Arabian peninsula associated with fate, fortune, and death. She is the oldest sister to Allat and Al-Uzza.
~~~~~~~~~~

Қазақ Қалпы

Қаз едік қатар ұшыб қаңқылдаған;
Сахара көлге қоныб салқындаған:
Бір өртке қаудан шыққан душар болыб,
Не қалды тәнімізде шарпылмаған.

Алаштың адамының бәрі мәлім:
Кім қалды таразыға тартылмаған;
Дегендер мен жақсымын толыб жатыр,
Жақсылық өз басынан артылмаған;

Тақылдаб, құр пысықсыб сөйлейтін көб,
Екпіндеб, ұшқыр атша қарқындаған;
Бос белбеу, босаң туған бозбала көб,
Киіздей шала басыб, қарпылмаған;

Еңкеңдеб ет аңдыған шалдар да көб,
Телміріб бір тойғанын ар қылмаған;
Ақ көңіл, алаң-бұлаң адамдар көб
Ішсе деб азын көбке, аңқылдаған;

Хайырсыз, неше сараң байлар да бар,
Қайықдай толқындағы қалтылдаған;
Бәрінен тыныш ұйықтаб жатқандар көб
Ұмтылыб талаб ойлаб талпынбаған;

Солардың қатарында біз де жүрміз
Мәз болыб құр түймеге жарқылдаған.
Не пайда өнерің мен біліміңнен,
Тиісті жерлеріне сарф ұрмаған.

Бұл бір сөз хасірет етіб, хатқа жазған.
Қалмаған түк қасиет, қазақ азған.
Байға мал, оқығанға шен мақсұд боб
Ойлайтын жұртдың қамын адам аздан.

~~~~~~~~~~
~~~~~~~~~~

Kazakhness

A goose might freeze flying, honking;
Landing in a dry lake, cooling.
A grass fire might break out,
Our bodies burned—what remains?

Alash's people all known:
Who was not measured?
Always saying, "I'm well,"
Wellness confined to themselves.

Chattering, feigning skilled speech,
Rushing, pushing, galloping;
Unbelted, a slack child coming
Like half-pressed felt, unfinished.

Hunched, old hunters seeking meat,
Searching, just one more honorable feast.
Sincere, they're here and there
Counting few to many, simple but generous.

Unhelping, many rich misers
Like boats on rocking waves.
So many lie silent, sleeping,
Moving without purpose or ambition.

We line up with them, orderly,
Satisfied with sparkling buttons.
What use from your talent,
If not struck in the right places?

These words, this letter I write with sorrow,
No value left, the lost Kazakh.
Rich worry wealth, educated worry rank,
Little worry left for the people.

~~~~~~~~~~
~~~~~~~~~~

Қазақ Салты

Қалтылдақ қайық мініб есбпесі жоқ,
Теңізде жүрміз қалқыб кешпесі жоқ.
Жел соқса, құйын қуса жылжи беру
Болғандай табан тіреу еш нәрсе жоқ.

Бұл күйге бүгін емес көбден кірдік;
Алды, артын аңдамаған бетбен кірдік;
Шығармай бір жеңнен қол, бір жерден сөз:
Алалық алты бақан дертбен кірдік.

Бейне бір құдіретді сынағандай,
«Сақтар деб, сақтар болса» сертбен жүрдік
Жат жақды жаратқанға күзеттіріб,
Жақынмен ырылдасдық итдей үрдік.

Білдірдік елдің сырын, ердің құнын,
Елеріб ерегіске екі-үш күндік.
Кіреді тентек есі түстен кейін
Мүшкілін халіміздің жаңа білдік.

Әлі де саңылаусыз салтын бағыб
Түрі жоқ іс айтетын пәлен дерлік;
Ұлы той «көббен көрген» жалғыз мен бе?
Деб отыр, не болса да жұртбен көрдік.

~~~~~~~~~~
~~~~~~~~~~

Kazakh Culture

Tremble aboard the boat adrift,
Glide across the sea, don't wade.
Forceful, maelstrom fed by currents,
Nothing fastened or ready.

Since, more have come;
Brash, mistaken, completely consumed;
Hands unjoined, scattered words,
This illness eclipsing even the Altybaqan.[*]

As if testing God's single form,
"Safety spoken, safety promised," an oath.
Far away, the Creator stands guard,
We growled, like dogs we barked.

We argued the country's secret, a man's value,
Disputes for two, three days.
A fool will realize too late;
Our new power brings hazards.

And yet, our tradition moves seamless,
Criticism speechless,
"Was I the only one to see the celebration?"
They say, "What comes, we see with our people."

~~~~~~~~~~~

----

[*]   Large swing made of six poles used in traditional Kazakh celebrations.
~~~~~~~~~~~

Достыма Хат

Қырағы қия жазбас сұңқарым-ай!
Қажымас қашық жолға тұлбарым-ай!
Үйілген өлексені өрге сүйреб,
Шығармақ қыр басына іңкәрім-ай!

Жарқыраб жақсылықдың таңы атбай тұр:
Түнерген төбемізден бұлт арылмай;
Көк етті, көн терілі, көніб қалған,
Сықса да шыдай беру жұрт жарылмай.

Кім біліб, ер еңбегін, сезіб жатыр?
Кім шыдаб жолдасдыққа төзіб жатыр?
Сасық ми, салқын жүрек санасыздар
Алаңсыз ақ малтасын езіб жатыр;

Сынайтын, жақсы менен жаманды өлшеб,
Құлдықдың қолдарында кезі жатыр;
Кешегі кеңшілікде керек қылған
Бостандық болмаған соң, безіб жатыр.

Айтқанмен таусылар ма оны-мұны?
Талайдың таңдамалы түпкі сыры:
Жанасқан шын көңілмен жақындық аз –
Көбінің іші салқын, сырты-ақ жылы;

Ақшаға абыройын арын сатыб
Азған жұрт адамшылық қалмай сыны;
Жаны ашыб жақын үшін қайғырар ма?
Жаны мал, жақыны мал, малдың құлы.

Letter to a Friend

My vigilant, all-seeing falcon!
My far-traveled, unrelenting warhorse!
Carrion gathered, pulled to pasture,
Your wanderlust still powerful!

A sun's bright blessing doesn't rise,
Clouds shrouding above, ceaseless.
Blued flesh, leather skin, in agreement,
If twisted in hardship, the people won't break.

Who knows, sensing a man's labor,
Who suffers, the partnership enduring?
Rotten brain, coldhearted,
Thoughtlessly preparing their meals.

Checked the good and bad, measuring,
Slavery's key in their hands,
They needed us when we were free.
Now with no liberty, we're abandoned.

Having said everything, will it end?
Few from several, basic truths:
Few sincerely joined together—
Warm in countenance, but cold within.

Selling honor for money, vices in trading,
The people lose, humanity absent.
Empathize, grieving for those close.
Are the greedy only slaves to wealth?

Жиған-терген

Ойұуын ойыб,
Орындаб қойыб,
    Түр салғандай өрнекке;
Қиыннан қиыб,
Қиырдан жиыб,
    Құраб, сөзді термекке,
    Еңбекке егіз, тіл мен жақ,
    Ерінбесең, сөйлеб бақ!
Имениб көбден,
Сақтық қыб еббен,
    Тасалама ойыңды!

Ашынса етің
Ашылмақ бетің,
    Тірі көмбей бойыңды,
    Жүрегіңнің жарасын
    Көрсет жұртқа! Қарасын:
Оқушым, ұқбай,
Осқырыб шықбай,
    Сабырмен байқа сөзімді!

Шыққан соң сыртқа,
Жайған соң жұртқа,
    Сөз тергеуге төзімді.
    Көб мағына аз ләфүз –
    Есек басбас тайғақ мұз.

Қарқылдар қарға,
Шиқылдар арба,
    Бой сүйсінер сазы жоқ.
Шешенсіб жұртқа,
Мылжыңдар қыртба,

Ой ісінер сөзі жоқ,
Маған үлгі ол емес;
Ол түсерлік жол емес.

Жолдар бар өзге;
Жоба бар сөзге,
    Жүрекке дөб, ойға жөн
Жаманды жаман
Демекпін һәман,
    Мейлің тұула, мейлің көн.
    Иланбасам, айтбаймын;
    Иманымнан қайтбаймын.

Һәр жолды ойлаб,
Ойыма бойлаб,
    Ұқтым тайыз тереңді.
Сайраған тілмен,
Зарлаған үнмен,
    Құлағы жоқ кереңді
    Ұқтыра алмай сөз әуре,
    Тек тұра алмай біз әуре.

Қараймын кейін:
Орысқа шейін
    Хан бағыбды қазақды.
Баға алмай жөндеб,
Басқаға көн деб,
    Артқан жұртқа азабды.
    Бас адамдар халықды
    Сатыб, сыйлар алыбды.

Келген соң бері.
Кейінгілері
    Болды құмар шекпенге
Өгіздей өрге,
Өткелсіз жерге
    Күнде айдаб жеккенге.
    Бір күн тойса есектер,
    Ми жоқ алдын есебтер.

Салыныб дауға,
Сатыныб жауға,
    Болысдықды алысды.
Қазық боб жұртқа,
Қорған боб сыртқа,
    Кім ойлады намысды?
    Мақтады ұлық (*) болды мәз!
    Қауым үшін қайғы аз.

Оқытды жасын,
Өстірдіб шашын,
    Мал табуға салынды.
Қаламнан хатдан,
Жауабдан айтқан.
    Білді жалғыз алымды.
    Кейбірі шен алмақ да,
    Дінін шаншыб қармаққа.

Басында сәллә,
Аузында Алла,
    Молдаларда не ғамал?
Көздерін сүзіб,
Жүздерін бұзыб.
    Алдаб жұртды жимақ мал.
    Ұжмақ молда қолында:
    Сауда-сатдық жолында.

Бергенге ұжмақ,
Бермесе дозақ,
    Деб үйретер халыққа.
Ұжмахтың кілтін,
Алланың мүлкін
    Арендаға (**) алыб па?
    Молда сатса тиынға,
    Ол Алла емес сыйынба!

---

*   ұлық – хәкім.
** Арендаға – жалдауға.

Шалқаңнан жатыб,
Алланы сатыб,
      Аламын деб қорлама!
Еңбексіз ит жер,
Бейнетсіз бит жер,
      Берсеңдер, бер молдаға!
      Өзіңді бірақ, алдама!
      Ақшаға ұжмақ жалдама!

Ұлғайыб қайғы,
Уытын жайды,
      Айтбасыма болмады.

~~~~~~~~~~

Қабағын түйіб,
Қаһарын жиыб,
      Жан жақды бұлт торлады.
      Жаңбыр жаумай, жауса қар,
      Жұрт жұтайтын түрі бар.

Балалық қалыб,
Ес біліб анық.
      Ер жеткелі жиырма жыл.
Байағы қалпы,
Байағы салты,
      Бұл неткен жұрт ұйқышыл?
      Болсын кедей, болсын бай,
      Жатыр бейқам, жым жырт жай.

Емшегін еміб,
Анаға сеніб,
      Бала ұйықтайды жасдықбен.
Қымызға қаныб,
Қызарыб жаныб,
      Бай ұйықтайды масдықбен.
      Шалаб ішкен кедей мас.
      Міне жұртдың түрі оңбас!
~~~~~~~~~~

Ұйқышыл жұртды,
Түксиген мұртты
    Обыр обыб, сорыб тұр.
Түн етіб күнін,
Көрсетбей мінін,
    Ойатқызбай қорыб тұр.
    Обыр болса қамқорың,
    Қайнағаны сол сорың!

Ойанған ерге
Ұмтылған жерде
    Еруші аз, серік кем.
Қас білген досды,
Дос білген қасды,
    Мұндай елді көріб пе ең?
    Қыс ішінде бірер қаз
    Келгенменен, қайда жаз!

Қазағым, елім!*
Қайқайыб белің
    Сынуға тұр тайаныб.
Талауда малың,
Қамауда жаның,
    Аш, көзіңді, Ойаныб!
    Қанған жоқ па әлі ұйқың?
    Ұйықтайтын бар не сиқың?!

~~~~~~~~~

---

*   Соңғы сегіз жол өлең төңкерісден бұрын шыққан «Маса»-лар-да сензура рұхсат етбегендіқден басылмаған. Б.К.
~~~~~~~~~

Pieces, Gathered

Thinking through design,
Its purpose, placing,
    As if ornamented,
Difficulty trimmed,
Gathered from afar,
    Forming, speech embroidered,
    Labor twinned with tongue and jaw,
    Don't be listless, speak!
Intimidated too long,
Cautious, skilled,
    Don't shroud your mind!

If your muscles burn,
Reveal yourself,
    Don't hide your dignity,
    Reconcile your heart,
Let them look.
Children, you misunderstand,
But don't scoff,
    Patience, listen!

After riding from a village,
After spreading to the people,
    The words resilient to criticism.
    Much meaning, little uttered,
    An ass wouldn't step on slippery ice.

The crow will caw,
The cart will creak,
    But a melody won't be admired.
Feigned eloquence to the people,
Gossipers stop chattering,
    Your words have no value.

To me, that is not the standard,
That is not the dream.

There are other paths,
There are plans spoken
    To the heart, apt for the mind.
Evil is evil,
As I will always say,
    Go mad or agree: either's fine.
    If I waiver, I won't say,
    I'll never betray my integrity.

All paths considered,
My thoughts grow,
    Learning depths and shoals.
Tongues chirping,
Voices cried
    To an unwilling ear.
    Words are insufficient,
    We can't just do nothing.

I will look back:
Before Russia
    The Khan raised the Kazakhs.
Not taking care,
A kind of ore,
    The people grew thin.
    Their leaders
    Mining them, profiting.

After they all came,
Their followers
    Impassioned in fine robes
To the hill as an ox,
To the pathless place
    Driven daily in the field.
    They keep the beasts well fed,
    Chewing instead of speaking.

Claims placed,
Sold to foes
    For positions, ranks.
Support for the nation,
Protection for the borders,
    Who thought to have honor?
    The greats praised, joyous,
    Little grief for the nation.

They instructed their youth
With unkempt hair,
    New wealth earned.
From the pen, the letter,
Answers spoken,
    Only gifts learned.
    Maybe a rank will be taken,
    Betraying beliefs.

Turbaned head,
God in their mouths,
    What do imams do?
Their eyes goring,
Faces breaking,
    Deceiving the people, gathering livestock.
    Heaven in a hand of the imam,
    Coin in the other.

"Having given—Heaven,
Having not—Hell,"
    Say the teachers to the people.
Heaven's key to
God's property,
    Did they rent?
    If the imam profits,
    He is not God, give him no respect!

Lying around,
Purchasing God,
    Don't say shamelessly!
A lazy dog's place,
A louse's idle seat,
    All of you give, give to the imam!
    But don't deceive yourself!
    You can't buy your way to Heaven!

Grief magnified,
Bitterness spread,
    I couldn't stay silent.

~~~~~~~~~~

Brow beats,
Anger gathers,
    Clouds blanket, surround.
    If the rain won't come, maybe snow,
    Famine's form looms.

Leaving childhood,
Becoming conscious,
    An adult for twenty years.
Forever static,
Forever set,
    Have they always slept?
    If poor, if rich,
    Lying absent, silent, calm.

Suckling the breast,
Trusting the mother,
    Child asleep.
Quench your thirst with qymyz,[*]

---

[*]   An alcoholic beverage made of fermented mare's milk.
~~~~~~~~~~

Redden, catch fire,
    The wealthy's drunken sleep,
    The poor flushed from shalap,*
    This nation won't last long!

Sluggish folk,
Stubbly mustached
    Gorger gluttoning, suckling.
Sleeping through the day,
Hiding their flaws,
    Not letting them wake.
    With the thoughts of a pig,
    You'll surely be unhappy!

Drawn to the place
Of the awoken man,
    A few followers, fellows.
The enemy knows the friend,
The friend the enemy,
    Have you seen such a nation?
    In winter even the goose
    Has come—but where is summer?

My Kazakhs, my people,**
Your bending back,
    Buckling, ready to break.
Your livestock plundered,
Soul trapped,
    Open your eyes. Wake up.
    Such restless sleep,
    What dreams keep you from living?

~~~~~~~~~~

---

*   Wine of low quality.
**   The last eight lines of the poem were not originally published due to censors.
~~~~~~~~~~

Анама Хат

Қарағым, дұғагөйім, қамқор анам!
Арнаб, хат жазайын деб, алдым қалам.
Сені онда, мені мұнда аман сақтаб
Көруге жазғай еді Хақ Тағалам!

Бара алмай, өтірікші болыб әбден,
Семейдің түрмесінде отыр балаң.
Мал ұрлаб, кісі өлтірген айыбы жоқ,
Өкімет өр зорлыққа не бар шараң?

«Үмітсіз шайтан болсын» деген сөз бар,
Жолдар көб жәннатқа да тарам-тарам.
Оқ тиіб он үшімде, ой түсіріб,
Бітбеген жүрегімде бар бір жарам.

Алданыб тамағыма, оны ұмытсам,
Болғандай жегенімнің бәрі арам.
Адамнан туыб, адам ісін етбей,
Ұйалмай, не бетіммен көрге барам?

Көб айтбай, қысқасынан сездіретін –
Балаңның мінезі бар сөзге сараң;
Кетер деб «суға құлаб, отқа түсіб»,
Қайғы жеб, менің үшін болма алаң!

Отырмын абақтының бөлмесінде
Бұйрықсыз көз жетеді өлмесіме.
Есікдің құлбы мықты, күзетші көб,
Ажалдан басқа һешкім келмесіне.

Қоршаулы айналасы биік қорған,
Берік қыб салған темір терезесіне.
Қалайша мұны көріб көңіл сенбес?
Аттаныб жау келсе де бермесіне.

Қаламда Лаухул Махфуз ұмытқан ба?
Жазбабды бұл орынды көрмесіме.
Қаңбақпен салмағың тең бұл бір заман –
Ылаж жоқ, жел айдаса ермесіне.

Тайпалған талай жорға, талай тұлпар,
Тағдырдың кез болыб тұр кермесіне.
Солардан жаным-тәнім ардақты емес,
Орынсыз күйзелейін мен несіне?

~~~~~~~~~~
~~~~~~~~~~

Letter to My Mother

I looked, pious patron mother!
This letter's for you, pen in hand.
You're there, I'm here, safe and sound,
God willing we'll see each other soon!

I can't go on holding this lie:
Your child was imprisoned in Semeĭ.
Not stealing a sheep, not killing a man,
But what power—what violence measured out!

"Only the devil's hopeless," they say,
Many roads branch to heaven.
At thirteen a bullet hit me, a fallen thought,
Unfinished wound within my heart.

Deceived by pleasantries, wounds forgotten,
But all of it impure.
Born from man, but no humanity,
Will I go brazen to my grave?

I can't say much, just small hints—
Your son is a hoarder of words:
I'll leave, "Fall into water, descend into fire,"
It's my sorrow, not yours to worry!

Sitting in prison, rooms undivided,
Unknown orders, sure I could die.
A door's strong lock, many guards,
Only death can come.

Enclosed, standing tall,
Barred windows,
How you wouldn't believe
Even enemies couldn't break through.

Did the pen forget destiny,[*]
My fate written to this unknown place?
Like a dandelion never still,
A gentle wind moving you.

Beauty in its gait, its gallop,
Destiny training, whipping.
My soul and body not better than those,
No right or reason to distress!

~~~~~~~~~~

---

[*] Al-Lawhu 'l-Mahfuz, "The Preserved Tablet," a heavenly record written by God recording all past and future events.
~~~~~~~~~~

Тілек Батам

Иә Хұдайым аққа жақ,
Өзіңе айан мен нахақ.
    Аққа деген жолымның
    Абыройын ашбай, жаб!

Айат пенен хадисде
Адал ниет ақ іске,
    Жаңылмасам, жоқ еді
    Жаза тартсын деген баб.
Мені ұстатыб, айдатыб,
Зығырданды қайнатыб,
    Масайрасыб, мәз болыб,
    Қуанғанды өзің таб!
Аз күндікке алданыб,
Аз нәрсеге жалданыб,
    Адасқанын Алаштың
    Түзу жолға түсір, хақ!

Жақын жерден жау шығыб,
Мақұл сөзден дау шығыб,
    Дұшпан ұстаб қолымнан,
    Итдер тістеб тонымнан,
    Маған тосу болған шақ.

Тұтқын болыб тарығыб,
Жалғыз жатыб зарығыб,
    Ашу қысыб, ойды алыб,
    Өт жайылыб, бойды алыб,
    Дерт жүрекке толған шақ.

Қатты айтды деб кекдемей,
Сыйынғанды тек демей,
    Он екі имам әулие
    Жиырма сегіз әнбие,
    Қолда өңшең аруақ!

~~~~~~~~~~

Қара балуан, Жәнібек!
Қаз дауысты Қазыбек!
    Жетім қалған халқыңа,
    Тұлға болыб артыңа,
    Кім тианақ қазық ед?

Құнсыз болыб еріміз,
Жесір болыб жеріміз,
    «Жан менікі» дей алмай,
    «Мал менікі» дей алмай,
    Ит пен құсқа азық ек.

Барын салыб таласқа,
Арын сатыб қалашқа,
    «Жұрт болалық» деген жоқ,
    Жұрт қайғысын жеген жоқ,
    Іріб, шіріб азыб ек.

Мұны көріб көзіміз;
Бірігер деб сөзіміз;
    Кен болар деб балшықты,
    Көл болар деб шалшықты,
    Біз үмітбен қазыб ек.
Дәреті жоқ айақдар,
Қорсылдаған сайақдар
    Былғамасын қасыңды,
    Қасиетті басыңды,
    Дегеніміз болмаса,
~~~~~~~~~~

Қазаққа не жазыб ек?
Байлаттырған қолымды,
Бөгеттірген жолымды,
    Жақыным бар, жатым бар,
    Хабарлана жатыңдар!
    Мен сендерге жүгіндім,
    Төресі әділ қазы деб!

~~~~~~~~~~
~~~~~~~~~~

My Prayer

Yes, my God is true,
Yourself known: I'm guiltless.
    My way of truth,
    Reputation hidden, sealed!

In the verse and in the hadith[*]
For clear intentions, honest work
    If I'm not mistaken,
    No need for punishment.
Seized, drive out my
Boiling rage,
    Celebrate, there's joy,
    Find this delight yourself!
Deceived by a brief day,
Work for small things,
    The lost of Alash
    Return to the correct way: truth!

The enemy appears nearby,
Argument after agreement,
    He grabs my hands,
    Dogs biting my coat,
    My time to wait.

Captured, wanting,
Lying, yearning, alone,
    Anger clenching, thoughts racing,
    Bile expanding, body consumed,
    Heart diseased.

---

[*]   Transmitted reports attributed to what the Islamic Prophet Muhammad said and did.

Harshly spoken, don't accuse me,
Praying for relief,
    Twelve holy imams,
    Twenty-eight saints,
    Please support us, our souls!

~~~~~~~~~~

Black wrestler Zhănibek!*
Goose-throated Qazybek!**
    Orphans of the people,
    Widows falling behind,
    Who will support them?

Our men lost their value,
Our land widowed,
    "My own soul," we can't say,
    "My own flock," we can't say,
    Rations of dogs and birds.

All towards argument,
Sell honesty for bread,
    "United," unsaid,
    Not suffering with people, hungry,
    We were sick, we waned.

We see with our eyes,
Our words might unite,
    That clay might be ore,
    A puddle, a lake,
    We dig with hope.

---

*   Zhănibek Khan was the second khan of the Kazakh Khanate from 1473 to 1480 and direct descendant of Genghis Khan. He was highly regarded for his wisdom.

**   Qazybek Biï was an elected Biï of the Orta Zhŭz clan in the early to mid-eighteenth century highly regarded for his wisdom and knowledge of songs and folk tales.
~~~~~~~~~~

Unwashed feet,
Geldings grunting,
    Not sully your surroundings,
    Your valued self!
    Rather than this,
    What did we do to Kazakhs?
My hands bound,
Road blocked,
    Friends near and unfamiliar far,
    We keep in touch!
    I trust you,
    Just judges!

~~~~~~~~~~
~~~~~~~~~~

Жауға Түскеннің Сөзі

Жанға көңіл қалыб тұр:
    Жан бұл күйге салыб тұр.
Тәнге көңіл қалыб тұр:
    Тән шыдамай арыб тұр.
Жұртқа көңіл қалыб тұр:
    Жұрт жалғанға наныб тұр,
Өтірік өрлеб күшейіб,
    Шын жеңіліб талыб тұр.
Бақ дегенге байлау жоқ:
    Уағдадан таныб тұр;
Тағдыр шіркін таб беріб,
    Тамағымнан алыб тұр;
Бәле деген аңдушы
    Айағымнан шалыб тұр;
Жала деген төбеті
    Балтырымнан қабыб тұр;
Жау білегін сыбанып,
    Пышағын қайраб, жаныб тұр.
Сауысқан, қарға, қарақұс,
    Жемтік аңдыб, бағыб тұр;
Көре алмаған күншілдің
    Көңіліне мұным жағыб тұр;
Табалаған жаманның
    Шайан тілі шағыб тұр;
«Әй сені ме!» дегеннің
    Айызы әбден қаныб тұр;
Жаны ашыған жақынның
    Жас көзінен ағыб тұр;
Айыруға амал жоқ,
    Қылышын жерге шауыб тұр.
«Әлдеқалай болар» деб,
    Жүрегі жұлқыб қағыб тұр;

Түгі жылы, білмедім:
    Түледі ме? Нағыб тұр?
Түлемеген түпкі дос,
    Түлегенің барыб тұр!..

~~~~~~~~~~
~~~~~~~~~~

Words of the Captive

Let down by the spirit:
    Drowning in this feeling,
Let down by the body:
    Not resilient, weak.
Let down by the people:
    Trusting in lies.
Lies rise in power,
    Truth defeated, exhausted.
Fortune unbound:
    A promise broken.
Fate forsaken,
    Choking me.
Disaster, the hunter,
    Feet tripping.
Misfortune, his dog
    Biting at my heels.
The foe rolls his sleeves,
    Knife sharpened, fired.
Of scabs, the crow, the vulture,
    Foraging, grazing, hunting.
People who envy me,
    Happy because of this,
Masochistic evil
    Scorpion tongues stinging,
"Just you wait!" their call,
    Pleased in my hardships.
Compassionate friends
    With tears in their eyes.
No way to divide,
    Blades ready,
"Fearing death,"
    Hearts pounding . . .

Warm hide, I didn't know,
    Molting? Is it true?
Unyielding honest friends,
    The changed can walk! . . .

~~~~~~~~~~
~~~~~~~~~~

Адамдық Диқаншысы

Адамдық диқаншысы қырға шықтым
Көлі жоқ, көгалы жоқ қырға шықтым
Тұқымын адамдықтың шаштым, ектім
Көңілін көгертуге құл халықтың.

Қор болған босқа кетіб еңбек, бейнет,
Құлдарға құлдықтан жоқ артық зейнет.
Оттай бер! Жануарым, екі айақты;
Адамдық хайуанға қанша қажет!

Жаратқан малды Хұдай не керекке?
Мінуге, сойұу, соғу, жүндемекке?
Жорта бер қамыт кииб, қамшыңды жеб,
Бұйрық жоқ ұрасың деб үндемекке.

Тайаққа еті үйренген қойшы жайлаб,
Көк есек қозғала ма? Түрткенге айдаб.
Есебден алданғандай болғандар көб
Жасықды асыл ма деб білмей қайраб.

~~~~~~~~~~
~~~~~~~~~~

A Farmer of Humanity

———————————

A farmer of humanity, I left for the hills.
No lake, no meadow to visit in vain.
Seeds of my benevolence I dispersed, cultivated,
To please the nation of servants.

Livestock worked to death, tormented,
Slaves beauty-less in servitude.
Incite, my two-legged animal,
How much humanity do beasts need!

Why did God create the animal?
To ride, to slaughter, to beat, to shear?
To trot with halter, to be flogged,
Afraid of your beating, no commands needed.

Numb to the shepherd's stick at pasture,
Will the donkey be moved by anything?
We've grown deceived,
Thinking we can polish meat like stone.

~~~~~~~~~~~
~~~~~~~~~~~

Көк Есекдерге

Не жазыб ем, Хұдай-ау, мен қазаққа?!
Мүбтала ғыб салғандай бұл азабқа.
Адамшылық есебіне кірісіб,
Қолы жетсін дегендік бе азадқа?

Жөн көрсетдім қазақ деген намысқа.
Жол сілтедім жақын емес алысқа.
Өзге жұртдар өрге қадам басқанда.
Дедім: сен де қатарыңнан қалысба!

Бар ма қазақ мұнан басқа қылғаным?
Ненді шаштым ненді бұздым былғадым?
Аштан өлген аталарың бар ма еді?
Тамақ үшін сатқан итдер иманын.

Көң тасыған көк есекдер, бәріңе,
Қалдырмастан жағалай жас, кәріңе,
Үрім бұтақ нәсіліңе қалғандай
Нық басылар кетбейтін мөр тәніңе.

Берінді де іздеб қараб көрермін;
Табқанымды тастамасбын терермін;
Миллат үшін еңбекдері сіңген деб,
Өсиет қыб кейінгіге берермін.

Асықбаңдар! Артымызда қазы бар.
Тергеб талай сүйектерің қазылар.
Пайғамбарды сатыб отыр тілла алған,
Йаһудамен бірге атдарың жазылар

Қинамайды абақтыға жабқаны;
Қиын емес дарға асқаны, атқаны;
Маған ауыр осылардың бәрінен.
Өз ауылымның итдері үріб қабқаны.

To the Blue Asses

What did I do, my Lord, to Kazakhs!
To have placed this torment,
To have entered humanity,
Mustn't they reach freedom?

I showed the Kazakhs honor.
I gave directions to the road afar.
When other peoples stepped up their hill.
I said: "Don't be left behind!"

Kazakh, did I do something besides this?
What did I break or soil?
Did your ancestors die from hunger?
Dogs selling their iman* for food.

Donkeys passing manure, all of you,
No exceptions for young or old.
Sprouts on a branch of your lineage,
Marks pressed into your flesh.

I'll search and see you all;
I'll collect and not toss my findings;
Saying your labor's done for the country,
I'll give this wisdom to those who follow.

---

*   Literally "faith" or "belief" in Arabic. Refers to the foundational Islamic belief in the Six Pillars of faith.

    Don't rush! There is a court behind us.[*]
You will be judged when your bones unearth.
Those who took money betrayed the Prophet,
Your names will be written next to the Jews.[**]

    Not tortured when imprisoned;
No difficulty in hanging, being shot;
Above all of these things,
The curs of my countryside bit hardest.

---

[*]   An Islamic court that resolves disputes according to sharia law.
[**]   Probably referring to the three main Jewish tribes of Medina who resisted conversion to Islam in the seventh century: the Banu Nadir, the Banu Qainuqa, and the Banu Qurayza. While some tribes were hostile to Islam, others lived peacefully under Islamic rule until the Invasion of Banu Qurayza in 627 CE when Jewish men, women, and children were either enslaved or executed.

Қа . . . қаласына

Хош! Сау бол, Қа . . . жуылмаған!
Айдай бер қалса адамың қуылмаған.
      Әдебді сыпайы елдің қалпібында жоқ
Жасырын дыбыс шықды шуылдаған.

      Бүркеніб арсыздарың шайнауына
Жем табды пісірмеген қуырмаған.
Шыққан соң талғамайтын доңыздарың
Қасыңа қиын болар жуу маған.

~~~~~~~~~~
~~~~~~~~~~

To the City of Qa------[*]

Goodbye! Farewell, filthy Qa------,
Go out, you've pushed away the remaining few.
Not what polite, modest people do,
Noise reeking hidden sources.

Covered, shameless chewing,
Grain found unboiled, unroasted.
After leaving, not being a picky pig,
It will be difficult to approach your stench.

~~~~~~~~~~

---

[*]   Qarqaral.
~~~~~~~~~~

Жұртыма

Бірлік қыб іс етуге шорқақ жұртым!
Табылса оңай олжа ортақ, жұртым!
Сиақты қара қарға шуылдаған
Үрейсіз, қойан жүрек қорқақ, жұртым!

Білмейсің жөнің менен терісіңді,
Ел болыб іс етбейсін келісімді.
Үміт қыб бәйге атындай талай қосыб,
Байқадық шабыс түгіл желісіңді;

Жөн айтқан жұртшылыққа адам болса,
Шығасын қолыңа ала керісіңді;
Бытыраб бет-бетіңе жөнелгенде,
Көрдік қой жайылатын өрісіңді;

Келгенде өзді-өзіңе мықты-ақсыңдар,
Қайтейін өзге десе көнгішіңді!
Сықылды сынық бұтақ төмендесең
Кім жұлмас оңайдағы жемісіңді?

~~~~~~~~~~
~~~~~~~~~~

To My People

You've never united, my people!
But treasure is easily found together.
You're noisy black crows,
Soulless rabbits, cowardly hearts!

Not knowing right from wrong,
Refusing agreement.
High hopes for trophies,
We saw your gallop slow to trot.

If one speaks true,
You'll fight with argument.
Wandering directionless,
We watched sheep graze.

Stubborn to your own people,
Why be friendly to others!
If like a hanging branch,
Who wouldn't claim your fruit?

~~~~~~~~~~
~~~~~~~~~~

Жұбатұу

Әлди-әлди, ақ бөпем!
Ақ бесікке жат, бөпем!
Жылама, бөбем, жылама,
Жілік шағыб берейін;
Байқұтанның құйрығын
Жібке тағыб берейін.
(Қазақдың бала жұбатұу өлеңі)

Қайран, еркін
    Замандарың!
Тарлыққа жоқ
    Амалдарың!
Еркін дала
    Еркін қайда!?
Еркіндегі
    Көркің қайда!?
Нұулы, нұулы
    Жерің қайда!?
Сұулы, сұулы
    Көлің қайда!?
Еркін көшкен
    Елің қайда!?
Ел қорғаны
    Ерің қайда!?
Тұура айтатын
    Биің қайда!?
Би бардағы
    Күйің қайда!?
Адал көңіл
    Андың қайда!?
Жалған антдан
    Сақдық қайда!?

Бауыр тартқан
	Жүрек қайда!?
Намыс қызған
	Сүйек қайда!?
Нұулы жерден
	Күшті айырды,
Сұулы көлден
	Сұсты айырды.
Ер орнына
	Еркек қалды;
Көлеңкеден
	Үркек қалды;
Би орнына
	Биің болды;
Би деу бірақ
	Қиын болды,
Қаралды би
	Жақтау болды;
Қараны жан
	Ақтау болды;
Бауыр, жүрек
	Талас боб тұр;
Намыс, сүйек
	Қалаш боб тұр.
Малың алдау,
	Талауда тұр;
Жаның арбау,
	Қамауда тұр;
Айағыңды
	Тұсау қысды,
Жақтарыңды
	Құрсау қысды.
Көрмесіңе
	Пердең мықты;
Өтбесіңе
	Кермең мықты;
Енді жатыб
	Ұйықтау қалды,

Ұйықтағанды
      Мақтау қалды
«Әлди-әлди!»
      Деб тербеткен,
Ұйықтасын деб.
      Көб тербеткен,
Қарның ашса
      Ұлықтарың
Жілік шағыб
      Май бермекші;
Тонсаң түлкі
      Құйрықтарын
Жібке тағыб
      Бай бермекші.
Әлди-әлди!
      Мен де деймін;
Сірә, «әлдиге»
      Сенбе деймін.

~~~~~~~~~~
~~~~~~~~~~

To Calm

Lullaby, lullaby, my little baby,
Lie in your white cradle, my little baby.
Don't cry, don't cry.
I'll give you a bit of bone marrow mush.
I'll give you a crane's feather
Tied to a string.
(Kazakh lullaby for children)

Surprise, free
    Your times!
Not limit
    Your deeds!
Free as the steppe
    Free where?
Feeling free
    Where is your beauty?
Foresty, foresty
    Where can you be?
Watery, watery
    Where is your lake?
Wandering, wandering
    Where is your land?
Country protected
    Where is your man?
Speaking true
    Where is your Biï?[*]
Biï's all here

---

[*] Biï were elected administrators and judges during the Kazakh Khanate era, generally
selected for their wisdom, knowledge, and eloquence.

Where is your kùĭ?*
Open hearted
    Where is your vow?
False oaths
    Where is your pause?
Longing for your brother
    Where is your heart?
Dignity ablaze
    Where is your bone?
Dense forest
    Split in strength,
Full lake
    Split in awe.
A man replaced
    A hero;
A coward
    Afraid of shadows;
Your Bĭ in place
    Another;
But difficult
    Calling them Bĭ,
Ill intentions
    Well supported;
Blackened souls
    Well protected;
Liver, heart
    Clash in thoughts;
Honor, bone
    Always at odds.
Cheat your flock,
    They bite and tear;
Your soul deceived,
    Stands imprisoned;
Your legs

---

*   A kùĭ is a Kazakh musical composition generally played by the dombyra, a long-necked
    two-stringed plucked instrument. Kùĭ tradition also includes a verbal component where
    the player first discusses the story being played regarding its historical context and distinct
    personality.

Laced and knotted,
Your sides
    Wrapped tight.
If you can't see
    Curtain dense;
Immobile
    Rope strong;
Now lie down
    Sleep comes,
Now sleeping
    Praises, lauds,

Lullaby, lullaby!
    Now swaying
To sleep,
    If hungry
Your leaders
    Mash marrow
Offer mush;
    If you're cold
Fox tails
    Tied to silk
The rich will give.

    Lullaby, lullaby!
I'll also say;
    Alas, don't trust
    this lullaby.

~~~~~~~~~~
~~~~~~~~~~

Н. Қ. Ханымға

Рақатсыз өтсе де өмір жасым,
Бұл жөнімнен Хұдайым айырмасын.
Ұзақ жолға ниет қыб бір шыққан соң,
Жарым жолдан қайтбасбын, қарындасым!

Сұу да болар ол жолда, тау да болар;
Жаудың оғы, жайған тор – ау да болар;
Мынау пайда, мынасы зиан демек,
Ол ерліктің ісі емес – сауда болар;

Шалдығатын, шаршайтын жерлер де бар.
Шалдыққанға мұқалмас ерлер де бар.
Қайратданыб қажымай тырмыссаң да,
Шыққызбайтын жолыңда өрлер де бар.

Шаршайды деб ойлама шалдыққаннан;
Ұзақсыныб жатбасбын жалыққаннан;
Жұрт, қолымнан келмесе, өкпелемес,
Барын сақтаб мен айаб алыб қалман.

Ел мұнымды білемін ұқпайтынын;
Көтермеге талғанда шықбайтынын;
Шалыс басыб айақды жығылғанда,
Жатқаныңнан тұрма деб мықтайтынын.

Мен өлсем де өлемін жөнімменен.
Тәннен басқа немді алар өлім менен.
Өлген күні абарыб тығары көр,
Мен жоқ болман көміліб тәнімменен.

Тән көмілер, көмілмес еткен ісім;
Ойлайтындар мен емес бір күнгісін;
Жұрт ұқбаса, ұқпасын жабықбаймын:
Ел бүгіншіл, менікі ертеңгі үшін.

To Mrs. N. K.[*]

Life passing my youth blisslessly,
From my course, my God won't deter.
Intentions made on the long road,
I won't return halfway, little sister!

Perhaps rivers along this road, mountains,
An enemy's bullet, a hidden trap—a net.
One's useful, one's harmful,
It's not a brave thing—but savvy.

Diseased, fatigue follows you,
But there are ill men still vigorous.
Even if strong and relentless,
Others will block the path.

Don't think I'll tire from illness,
Going far, not stuck in boredom.
People, if I'm unable, don't resent,
Hold everything, hoard, I won't do it.

I know this country doesn't understand,
Exhausted after hiking this peak,
Legs sore from tripping, falling,
"Don't get up!" holding tight.

If I die, I'll die on my course,
What else but my body could death steal?
The day of death carried hiding a grave,
I won't be buried with my body.

---

*   Written to Nazipa Qūlzhanova, the first Kazakh woman to become a journalist and
frequent contributor to *Kazakh.*

Flesh interred, perhaps not my work,
Thinking not only of today.
If they don't understand, they don't, I won't be offended:
The country lives today, I'll be here for tomorrow.

Ақын Ініме

Азырақ сөзге құлағың сал, ақын інім!
Ойымыз, рухымыз жақын, інім!
Ағалық правасын қолыма алыб,
Келемін айтайын деб, ақыл інім!

Өзімді ағаңмын деб үлкейтемін;
Онымды көремісін мақұл, інім!
Адасқан ағаңыздың жері болса,
Тілеймін ете гөр деб ғафұу, інім!

Жай жатсаң жаңылмайсын, адасбайсын,
Күресде кім кетбейді қабыл, інім!
Ат қойған аз көбіне қарамастан,
Ақылға біздер жарлы, фақыр, інім!

Доңыздай талғамай жеб семіргендер,
Саналыб ақылдыға жатыр, інім!
Сүйікті милләтыңа болам десең,
Нашардың көбірек же, хақын інім!

Сыйласын десең жұртың қадір тұтыб,
Айғырсыб момындарға ақыр, інім!
Білімді ел ішінде болам десең,
Шешенсіб жоқды сөйлеб лабыр, інім!

Қолыңнан мұның бірі келмес болса,
Кісімсіб ең болмаса қақыр, інім!
Сөзіңді тыңдатайын десең жұртқа,
Ет асыб табақ-табақ шақыр, інім!
Аузымен орақ орыб бәрін де етер,
Қымызды шара-шара сабыр, інім.

Ет пенен қымыз беріб, сөйлеб көрсең,
Айтқаның жұртқа балдай татыр, інім!
Ақылың Афлатондай болсадағы,
Қымыз бен еті жоқ құр татыр білім.

~~~~~~~~~~
~~~~~~~~~~

To My Little Brother Poet[*]

Lend your ear, brother poet,
Thoughts, opinions, spirits close, my brother.
"The elder brother's right to take,
To come and speak,"—smart, brother!

"I am your brother,"—I'll show you,
Please accept it, my brother.
If I'm lost or mistaken,
I pray you'll forgive me, brother.

If you do nothing, you won't mistake, lose your way,
Who will not regret in the struggle, my brother.
Naming few or many doesn't matter,^{**}
Our minds destitute, my brother.

Those like pigs eating anything, fattening,
Considered intelligent, my brother.
If you want to be beloved by your country,
Protect the truth of the poor, my brother.

If you want your people to honor you,
Take control, shout to the obedient, my brother.
To be educated in this country,
Adopt sophistry, say nothing, my brother.

---

* Written to Mīrzhaqyp Dulatov, a Kazakh poet, writer, and fellow member of the Alash Orda government.

** Referring to the Muslim practice of the eldest son inheriting the parents' property and wealth.

If you can't do any of this,
Be aloof and spit down, my brother.
If you want the people to listen to you,
Invite them to dine with you, my brother.
Their mouths could cut like a sickle, do everything,
Pour qymyz bowl to bowl, my brother.

If you give them meat and qymyz and talk with them,
Your words will be as sweet as honey, my brother.
Even if your wisdom could be like Plato,
Without qymyz, without meat, it's useless.

~~~~~~~~~~
~~~~~~~~~~

И. Б. Жездем Хатынан

Тұрмысың жырақ,
Аман ба? Шырақ!
Күйзелібсін көбірек,
Милләт үшін бегірек.
    Һәмәнда сақтан!
    Сақтамақ Хақдан,
Қоршаған дұшбан төңірек.

Милләтке қызмет,
Жұмлаңа міндет.
Ұйқыны аш! дер ек,
Надандықтан қаш! дер ек.
    Болмайды үндеб:
    Дұсбан тұр күндеб,
Бізде бұл бір індет.

Әр сөзің алтын.
Ұғар ма екен халқың?
Сынаған да шығарсын
Милләтдің қалпын.
Тіл алмас деб қорқамын,
Дер едім тартын.

    ~~~~~~~~~~

Мода(*) болды кіділік.
Сал сөзді елегіш.
Бір жөнге тарту жоқ;
Шалқайақ ерегіс,

    ~~~~~~~~~~

Алалықдан күш бөлу,
Бұл қанша керек іс?
　　Шемен бар әуе дерлік;
　　Сасық бар бүйе дерлік;

　　　~~~~~~~~~~

Замана түрленді,
　　Жақсылар кірленді,
Азасынан ұу жерлік

　　. . . . .

　　　~~~~~~~~~~

Letter From My Brother-in-Law, I. B.

———————

You're far away,
Are you well, dear!
If you've grown depressed,
Be strong for your country.
    Always careful,
      Protective of the people
Envious villains surround.

Serving the nation,
Everyone obliged.
Wake up, we say,
Abandon ignorance, we say.
    Can't speak up.
    Enemies covetous,
It's our disease.

Your words golden,
Will the people understand?
You've tested them, I gather,
What the country's made of.
I fear they don't listen,
I would say give up.

    ~~~~~~~~~~

Honesty in vogue.
Filter your words.
No invitations to dignity;
Disputes everywhere,
Separate strengths divided,
    ~~~~~~~~~~

Is it really needed?
 Sorrow like clouds;
 Evil like spiders;

~~~~~~~~~~

Times change,
 The good corrupted,
Eating poison at funerals.[*]

. . . .

 ~~~~~~~~~~

---

[*] Funeral offerings given to the family by friends and relatives. Additional offerings can be made seven days, forty days, one hundred days, or more after the death, depending on local customs.

Жауаб Хатдан

Аманбыз, жезде!
Солай ма сізде?
Амандасбақ жол, әдет.
Тағзымға – тағзым,
Назымға – назым
Тілеушілік ол әдеб.
Жолдан мен де шықбайын,
Сөзбен сыйлаб мықтайын.

~~~~~~~~~~

Жолға сіз көсем,
Сөзге һәм шешен,
Оның менде бірі жоқ.
Іздемей жоғын,
Шайқамай тоғын,
Қараб жатқан тірі жоқ.
Мен де соның бірімін.
Өлгенім жоқ, тірімін.

Ағаның ақыл,
Айтқаны мақұл,
Жаны ашыған жақындық.
Мен жазған кеңес,
Мақтаныш емес
Ат шығармақ ақындық.
Ер батқанда жорғалық;
Молда жоқда молдалық!

~~~~~~~~~~

Байқасақ, жезде!
Бауыздар кезде
        Үн шығу бар емес пе!
Үндемей өлсек,
Сүйекпен көмсек,
        Кейінгілер демес пе:
Ұлақ құрлы бақырмай,
Өлген екен, апырмай!

~~~~~~~~~~

«Милләтке қызмет,
Бәріңе міндет».
        Деб айтасыз өзіңіз.
Милләтден безұу
Әйтбесе төзұу,
        Шын болса сол сөзіңіз.

Кей іс шарты құрбанмен,
Болмас қорқыб тұрғанмен.

~~~~~~~~~~

Мен бұқтым, жатдым,
Сен бұқтың, жатдың,
        Кім істемек қызмет?
Ауызбен айтыб,
Істерге қайтіб.
        Жоламасақ не міндет?
Тек жүрсе, тоқ жүрмекді,
Қиын деме білмекті.

~~~~~~~~~~
~~~~~~~~~~

Жезде-еке, солай!
Көрмессіз қолай
    Жан сақтаудың ебіне.
Айтбайтын жыр бар,
Ашпайтын сыр бар
    Тымақтының көбіне.
Сізге жаздым ұғар деб,
Тымағы жоқ шығар деб.

. . . .

~~~~~~~~~~
~~~~~~~~~~

Reply to a Letter

We're well, brother-in-law,
And you?
I'll greet you—a path, habit.
Bow to bow,
Poem to poem,[*]
Sincerity—Politeness.
I won't leave this road,
Giving words of strength.

~~~~~~~~~~

You follow the path of a leader,
Your words of an orator,
I don't have these qualities!
Searching for nothingness,
Shaken by wealth,
No one sits idle!
I'm one of them,
I didn't die, but alive.

A brother's wisdom,
Accepting speech,
Compassion in closeness.
I've written advice,
Without arrogance,

----

[*]   Type of poetry written in Eastern tradition characterized by its playful manner and delicate feeling.
~~~~~~~~~~

Perhaps a poet renowned.
A man sinking—we will stroll,
Without imam—we'll do his work!

~~~~~~~~~~

Have you noticed, brother-in-law!
In the moment of slaughter,
     Is there not a cry?
Muted death,
Bones buried,
     Will the procession follow us?
Didn't wail like a baby goat,
Death arrived, oh no!

~~~~~~~~~~

"Service for the nation,
Everyone obliged."
     You said yourself.
Abandon your country,
Otherwise stay patient.
     There should be truth in your speech.

Some duties need sacrifices.[*]
We can't stand in doubt.

~~~~~~~~~~

I hide—I lie down,
You hide—you lie down,
     Who will do the work?

---

[*] Livestock used for ritual sacrifice.
~~~~~~~~~~

Speak up,
Return to work,
      If we don't, what's our job?
If you go quickly, you'll be satisfied,
Despite unknown difficulties.

~~~~~~~~~~

Brother-in-law, it's true,
Stretched convenience,
      Protect your soul from the wind.
There are songs unsung,
Secrets unopened
      For those wearing tymaqs.*
I write to you hoping you understand:
Thinking that you don't have one.

. . . .

~~~~~~~~~~

---

*   Traditional fox fur hat; a sign of distinction among early Kazakh communities.

Ғылым

Ғылымдар дүниалық сихыр болмақ;
Оқыған ол ғылымды кәфір болмақ;
Зулатыб шариғатды шарт жүгініб
Молдекең отырғанда мойнын толғаб.

Сондықтан заман жүйрік, біздер шабан;
Артында ілесе алмай жүрміз һәман;
Күн сайын өзгеріліб, өнер артыб,
Бәрі де бара жатыр алға таман.

«Заманың түлкі болса, тазы боб шал!»
Деген сөз айатбенен бірдей маған
Алақдаб артымызға қарағышдаб
Жүргенде-ақ озыб, ұзаб кетді заман;
Нәрсені түске енбеген өңде көрдік;
Соларды табқан ғылым, дейміз жаман.

Ғылым деб нені үйрендік біздер жасда
(Айтқаным бекер болса, алмай таста.
Табылар ақтайтын да, боқтайтын да,
Сөз емес арнаб жазған дос пен қасқа)

Ғылым бар бет жұуу да талай дедік;
Жұуған жөн былай бастаб, бұлай дедік;
Жұусандар солай етіб сауабы көб,
Жаза бар жумағанда олай дедік.

Шартдар көб дедік ғұсыл құйынғанда;
Шаһуат пәлендей боб құйылғанда;
Қалайша көзде . . . деб айтбады екен?
Үйрет деб мұның бәрін бұйырғанда!

Әйелмен пәлен бар деб жанасқанда;
Пәлен деб ұйқысыраб адасқанда;
Үйрету балаларға қандай жақсы!
Ақылға салыб, ойлаб, бал ашқанда!

Мектебде оқымаған білмей жүр ғой!
Жердегі мал-махұлық, құс асбанда?
Айтамын молдекең жоқ оңашада,
Сөз бермес кәфірсің деб таласқанда.

~~~~~~~~~~
~~~~~~~~~~

Science

"Sciences of the world like magic,
A student of science is a nonbeliever."
Quickly kneel to the sharia,
The imam giving his words.

That time was quick, we're behind,
Not always falling in line.
Changing daily, arts growing,
They all go forward.

"If time's a fox, catch it like a dog"—
Dogma is the same to me.
Glancing back, all around,
Running, time left us behind.
"We've seen undreamt of things,
Discovered by—science," we say wrongly.

What did we learn from "Science" in our youth?
(If I've said fiction, leave it!
Some will protect, some will curse,
Words not written for friends and enemies . . .)

There is science in washing our faces;
Beginning to clean in this way;
Follow cleanliness, it will bring blessings,
But punishment in not doing so.

Terms in pouring ablutions;[*]
The spilling of seed;
To focus . . . why didn't they say?
While they taught all this to everyone!

Some with women adjoin;
Some sleepwalk astray;
So good to teach the children!
Reflecting, thinking, guessing!

Those who didn't study don't know!
Beasts on the earth, birds in the sky?
I say none of us are like an imam,
In arguments about the godless.

~~~~~~~~~~

---

[*] Islamic ablutions required before prayer after certain acts such as defecation or sexual
intercourse.
~~~~~~~~~~

Надсоннан

Шайылған көз жасымен жердің бетін
Өткізіб, тым өлшеусіз, өкіметін
    Жауыздық жалғандықпен қабдағанға;
Адал жол, ақ ниетді, арам жеңіб,
Жазықсыз жанды қинаб, қанды төгіб
    Бұзықдық, түзікдікді табтағанға;
Қиналыб, кім болсаң да, талыққандар,
Түңіліб, үміт үзіб жабықпаңдар!
Қайтадан жақындық кеб, қасдық қашыб,
Жарқыраб жақсылыққа атар таң бар.

~~~~~~~~~~

Еңкейіб еңсесіне бейнет артбай,
Шөгер тәж шынжыр кииб, азаб тартбай,
    Жақындық келер күшті сәулетінде;
Көз жасы, тірі мола, құлдық, хорлық,
Дар-ағаш, қылыш – қанжар, өшдік, зорлық,
    Бірі жоқ жақындықдың дәулетінде;
Жанға жұт, жарық сәуле, жоқ мұқтаждық,
Сырт берер адамзатдың әулетіне;
Артықша тасқан қайтыб, толған солыб,
Құритын кез келмекші нәубетіне.

~~~~~~~~~~

Демендер! Жақсылық таң жай үміт құр,
Заман тар, жауыздық зор, тым қысыб тұр,
    Айналаң қараңғы түн, тым түнерген.
Қиналыб, талар дүниа азаб шегіб,
Қалжырар жалмауыздар қанға бөгіб,
    Болдырар, алыс-жұлыс жұлына ерген.

Жүре алмай, дымы құрыб сонда әрі,
Соқпалы, содыр жолдан шығар бәрі;
Талған күш, қиналған тән, ауырған жан,
Дертіне жақындықты етер дәрі.

~~~~~~~~~~
~~~~~~~~~~

From Nadson[*]

The ground washed of tears
Passing immeasurable authority
    To those covered in wickedness and falsity;
Filth overcoming the true path, honest intentions,
An innocent soul tortured, blood spilt
    To the trampled in sunken debauchery;
Suffering, who could be, the exhausted,
Don't despair, hope torn from the hopeful!
But again, nearness comes, ending opposition,
A shining virtue dawns.

~~~~~~~~~~

Not working too much, not loaded,
Not knelt with chains, not suffered,
    Nearness will come in its glory;
Tears, living grave, slavery, humiliation,
Gallows, sword-dagger, vengeance, violence,
    Not a one in the power of closeness;
Souls not starved,^{**} bright sunlight, no destitution,
Giving a good appearance to humanity's dynasty;
The abundant return, those filled will wilt,
There will be a time their disaster will disappear.

~~~~~~~~~~

---

*   Adapted to the Kazakh from Semyon Nadson's Russian version, "Друг мой, брат мой, усталый, страдающий брат…" (1880).

**   A massive loss of livestock from starvation, often as a result of harsh weather or the freezing of recently thawed pasture lands that prevent grazing.

Don't speak! Goodness is just a pointless hope,
Our time is harsh, vast villainy, pressured,
     Surrounded by darkness, blackest night.
Exhausted, tormented, the world suffers,
Weakened witches swelled of blood,
     Tired will be the one who follows the struggle.
     Can't walk further, losing everything,
All will leave this path of violence;
Strength drained, body suffering, soul sickened,
This illness, closeness, love is the cure.

~~~~~~~~~~~
~~~~~~~~~~~

Бақ

Бұлттар басыб жасырған,
Жана түсіб басылған,
      Таң шафағы сөніб тұр:
Жаңаланған өмірден,
Жаңа шығыб көрінген
      Гүл қамауда сеніб тұр.
Балалықтан басталыб.
(Тастаймын аз жасды алыб,
      Есіме нағыз енгенше)
Көрдім қызық, көрмедім?
Көрсем баға бермедім,
      Бозбала жас келгенше.
Құстай түлкі алатын,
Жайыб алтын қанатын,
      Уұылжыған от лепді
Жігіттік жас келді де
Ойды бір-аз бөлді де
      Тұрағы жоқ ол өтді.

Құудым бақды, іздедім.
«Табамын – ғой тез» дедім.
      Азаб шекті тән-жаным.

Қараб жақын жырақты,
Жақтым түрлі шырақты,
      Табдырмады қуғаным.

Үміт сүйрер жыраққа,
Жетесің деб мұратқа
      Талықсам да ізденіб.

Қашан көңіл жасарар?
Арқа басың босанар,
    Рақаты жаз келіб?

Қашан жаныб шамшырақ?
Сәуле беріб жарқыраб,
    Болар жарық төрт тараф?

Қашан маған іздеген
Күліб жылы жүзбенен,
    Болар серік бақ қараб?

Garden

Clouds concealed,
Shining settled down,
    The soft glow of dawn dies.
Life renewed,
New sprouts breaking
    Free of withered flowers.
Beginning from childhood,
(I'll throw a bit of my youth;
    I remember well)
I saw curiosities, didn't I?
Their unknown worth within
    Until I became a young man.
Like an eagle snatching a fox,
Gold wing unfolding,
    Great fire growing.
Seems like maturing comes
With sparse lucid thoughts,
    Also without refuge.

Driven from the garden, I searched,
"I'll go quick," I said,
    Body and soul suffering.

Looking near and far,
I ignited the flame,
    Unfound in exile.

Hope might drag you distant,
Reaching for ambition,
    I could tire in searching.

When in happy youth,
Our minds freed,
    Will a blissful summer come?

When the light burns,
Brilliant glow,
    Will the light grow?

When will it come,
Smiling with an earnest face,
    Fortune, as a friend?

Пұушкин Уалтерден

Қыздар дейсін тоб жиынды, жан дейсің,
Қыздыратын жасты қайдан ал дейсің?
Өмірімнің таңын қосыб кешіне
Бер қайтадан өткен күннің һәммесін!

Бере алмасаң, кең салалық бейілді;
Жас қызығын көрсін жастар кейінгі.
Тәтті өмірмен нәфсі көңілін ауладық,
Қалғанымен алданталық зейінді!

Уа, дарйға! Өтдің басдан, қызық жас!
Өсіңе жөн, өзгелерге бұзық жас.
Қайғы, Хасірет дертін жанға батырмай,
Қайран жастық! Қызуымен қылған мас!

Көрінбестен өмір көбі өткен шақ,
Тіршіліктің сән, ләззаты кеткен шақ.
Ойын күлкі, мәжілістен, қызықтан
Мезгіл құуыб: «Шық!» деб, әмір еткен шақ.

Жасың айтса, көнбегеннен не пайда?
Уақыттың тілі шолақ: «Жүр!», «айда!»
Тұрлауы жоқ, өзгерілгіш өмірдің
Өтбесіне еткен, сірә, кім айла!

Мүмкін десек адамзатқа екі өлмек,
Бірі соның – «жасым жетді» деб көнбек;
Бұл елімнің ардақтысы – аруы,
Мұнан кейін өлім-бе, сол дем сөнбек?!

~~~~~~~~~~
~~~~~~~~~~

Pushkin's Voltaire[*]

You think about revelry, lust, soul speaking,
From where can youth warm me, you ask?
My life's morning and night united
To give everything of yesterday again!

If you can't give with wide approval;
Young people should feel their youth.
With sweetened life we entertain our desires,
Misleading our conscience with what remains!

Oh, to the gallows! I've experienced a full youth!
For you it's okay, others see a young rebel.
Sadness, sorrow can't reach your soul,
Dear youth! Flushed with drunkenness!

Youth passed invisible,
Elegant existence, pleasure in the past,
From laughing at games, meetings, fun
Seasons come, "Go on!" said, by old edicts.

If age could speak, what could it tell you?
Time's trimmed tongue: "Go!" "Run!"
No dwelling, your changing life
To not pass, Oh, how to trick it!

Maybe it's said humanity has two deaths,
One "My youth's passed" said accepting;
This is my people's measure of honor, beauty,
Is it death after the breath's extinguished?!

~~~~~~~~~~

---

[*] Adapted to the Kazakh from Alexander Pushkin's Russian version, "Юность" (1826), which is a translation of Voltaire.
~~~~~~~~~~

Ат

Сен неге, тұлпар атым! Кісінейсің?
Жабығыб неден көңілің, түсді еңсең?
Ерігіб, ауыздығың қарш-қарш шайнаб,
Бұ қалай, бұрынғыдай сілкінбейсің?

Әлде мен, бабың тауыб, бақпадым-ба?!
Болмаса, жемнен қысыб, сақтадым-ба?
Әйтбесе, әбзелдерің сәнді емес пе?
Жібектен тізгініңді тақпадым-ба?
Малдырыб саф алтынға үзеңгіңді,
Тағаңды шын күмістен қақпадым-ба?

Жауабы иесіне берген атдың:
«Сұрайсың не сәбебден мен жабықтым,
Алыстан құлағыма келер дүбір
һәм дауысы керней тартыб, атқан оқдың.

Кісінеб себебім сол мен аһ ұрған:
Көб жүріб далада енді сейіл құрман.
Әбзелмен жарқыраған әсем басыб,
Аз қалды сыйлы, сынды күндер тұрған.

Жақында жаны ашымас жау кеб шабар;
Қалдырмай әбзелімнің бәрін тонар;
Соқтырған шын күмістен тағаларды;
Сұуырыб айағымнан, олжаланар.

Күйзеліб, жаным ашыб, ауырыб бек,
Қайғырыб, уайым ғыб, тұрмын жүдеб;
Орнына желбуіштің терінді әкеб,
Терлеген бүйіріме жабады деб».

~~~~~~~~~~
~~~~~~~~~~

Horse

My steed, why do you whinny?
Why does your head hang?
Restless, mouth chomping at the bit,
Why this, your mane unshaken?

Did I not tend to you?
Did I not feed and protect you?
Did I not praise your beautiful saddle?
Did I not tie your silk reins?
Your gilt stirrups and silver horseshoes,
Did I not hammer them?

The horse gives its sad answer:
"You ask why I frown?
My ears hear hooves approach from afar,
Horns blowing, bullets firing.

Why I whinny and sigh,
Days of strolling in fields are few.
Even adorned with glittering saddle,
I feel respect and beauty dwindle.

---

[*] This poem was initially published in *La Guzla* (1827), a translated collection of work by Hyacinthe Maglanovich of the Adriatic province of Illyria into French, by the French writer and poet Prosper Mérimée. Alexander Pushkin translated eleven poems from the French collection into Russian, including "Horse" (1833), before being notified by Mérimée through a friend that the translations were inauthentic and written by Mérimée with the exception of a single Serbian poem. Despite being inauthentic, Mérimée established a successful writing career and those works have since been further translated.

The unsouring enemy may soon attack,
May soon take everything from me,
May plunder the hammered silver
Horseshoes from my feet.

I'm worn thin: Broken down, soul-bared,
Ill, grieved, distressed.
I fear that instead of your blanket,
Your cold hide will be what covers
My sweating sides."

~~~~~~~~~~
~~~~~~~~~~

Данышпан Алекдін Ажалы

Жар салыб, жасақ жиар білімді Алек.
Білімсіз хұзарлардан алмаққа кек.
Қаласын, егіндерін ызасы үшін,
От пенен қойған арнаб қылышқа деб.
Қол бастаб, кииб сауыт – Тсаргградды,([*])
Сыр мінез таңдаб мініб сенімді атды.
Далада келе жатыб, кіназ көрді
Ішінен қалың орман шыққан қартты.

(^{**}) Перұнға көнген, берген ықыласын,
Болжаған болар заман уақйғасын,
Қасына Алек келді қарианың
Өткізген құлшылықпен, балмен жасын.

«Не болар, айтшы, бақсым! Хұдай сүйген;
Ілгергі өтер жасым нендей күймен?
Жауымды жан жақтағы құуандырыб,
Топырақ тез басар ма? Денеме үйген.

Ашыб айт! бүкпей бәрін, еш қаймықпа!
Аласың таңдаб жақсы ат айтқандыққа!».
– «Бақсылар кіназ сыйын қылмас хажет
Һәм қорықпас болғандардан ие жұртқа;

Олардың тілі еркін, сөзі хақ-ды,
Құдірет әмірімен ынтымақты
Қараңғы таңдағылар танытбайды
Жүзіңнен саған деген көрем бақды.

---

*   Тсарград – Ыстанбұл қаласының бұрынғы аты; Сауыт Тсарград – сонан шыққан сауыт.
**   Перұн – дінсіздер табынан бұт.

«Ұмытбай, ал жадыңа! Сөзін қартдың,
Батырға қымбат пұлы дабыс-даңкдың.
Атың зор, айбының мол жау мұқатқан
Қалқаның қақ басында Тсарграддың.

Айамай, берген саған бақ-талайды,
Күңіркеб, дұспандарың көре алмайды;
Жер сұу да, бәрі саған бағынулы,
Толқыны көк теңіздің ала алмайды;

Айбалта, оқ найза да, сом қанжар да,
Ешбірі саған залал қыла алмайды;
Астына көк сауытың жара түсбес,
Қорғаушың көрінбейтін бар бір сайлы.

Қатерлі не бейнеттен қорықпас атың;
Сезеді қозғалғанын, қалай таңым.
«Тұр!» десе жауған оққа қимылдамас
«Шұу!» десе не қамалға кірер батыл;

Сұуыққа, соғысқа да тұлпар шыдар;
Ажалың, бірақ осы аттан болар . . .»
Сөзіне шалдың айтқан күлді Алек,
Әйтсе де ой мен жүзі торғылданар.

Көңілсіз, ойдағы жоқ естіб ісді,
Үндемей, ерге асылыб аттан түсді.
Сипалаб, қасыб, қағыб мойынға атын,
Айнымас досбен кіназ хош айтысты:

«Бақыл бол, серік атым, ренжіме!
Айырылар мезгіл жетсе, айырмас не?
Дамыл ал! Хош аман бол! Мені ұмытба!
Айағым тимас алтын үзеңгіңе.

Келіңдер, бозбалалар, атды алыңдар!
Жетектеб, тоғайыма апарыңдар!

Жабыңдар! Жабуына түкті кілем;
Тазалаб, жуыб, бағыб, бабдаңыздар!

Жеміне ең қалаулы сұлы алыңдар!
Бұлақдың сұуымен һәм суарыңдар!»
Кіназға, атын алыб, тосды басқа ат;
Өтеді мұнан кейін неше жылдар.

~~~~~~~~~~

Басында бір қорғанның Алек тойлаб,
Жасақпен жанындағы күліб ойнаб,
Қайғы жоқ, хасірет жоқ, ішіб бәрі,
Күндерді бастан кешкен сөйлер ойға аб.

Ескерді бір мезгілде атын Алек,
Сұрайды: «Есен-сау ма һәм қайда? деб:
«Жүрісін, жүйріктігін танған жоқ ба?
Жабығыб қалмады ма?» дейді жүдеб».

Қайда деб, жоқтаған соң Алек атын,
Айтады біреу тұрыб: «Кіназ батыр!
Басында биік қырдың әлдеқашан;
Тыныштық алыб, атың ұйықтаб жатыр».

Мұны естіб, Алек жерге қараб төмен,
Ойлайды: «Отдаб босқа шал не жеген?!
Құу бақсы! Өтірікші, алжыған шал,
Атымды айырыбсын босқа менен».

Көруге атдың сүйек-сайақтарын,
Ертіб аб «Игор» менен қонақтарын,
Сарайдан шығыб, Алек келе жатыр,
Жағалаб Днепрдің (*) алабдарын.

---

* Днепр – өзеннің аты.
~~~~~~~~~~

Құуарған жатыр сүйек қыр басында,
Селеулер жел құбылтқан тұр басында.
Құм көмген, жаңбыр жуған сүйекдердің
Аралаб кіназ Алек жүр қасында.

Ақырын, айағын саб, шығыб басқа,
Сөз сөйлер, кіназ тұрыб өлген досқа:
«Жат, достым! Кәрі иеңнен қайтқан бұрын,
Құдірет қарамайды көб-аз жасқа.

Жазыбды сені асыма сойғызбасқа.
Қаныңмен топырағым тойғызбасқа.
«Ажалың атдан болар» деб сандалыб,
Шал мені қорқытқаны осы бас-па?!»

Білдірмей, бас ішінен жылжыб шығыб,
Кіназға қара жылан шабды ысқырыб.
Оралыб айағына, шаққан кезде,
Батырдан шықды дыбыс, жаны ышқыныб . . .

Алекді жоқтаб жұрты көб жылайды,
Өлген соң, жылағанға ол тұрмайды.
Днепр жағасында асын беріб,
Көбіршіб сабты айақдар быжылдайды.

Олга мен кіназ Игор дөң басында:
Тойлаған жасақдары һәм қасында:
Күндер, бастан кешкен сөйлей түсер,
Сабды айақ жүрген сайын ортасында . . .

~~~~~~~~~~
~~~~~~~~~~

The Death of Alek the Wise[*]

———————————

Alek the Wise announced to gather soldiers,
To take revenge on the ignorant Qazars.[**]
Their city, their crops, his rage demanded
Them to be burned and slashed.
To lead, wearing armor—to Tsargrad.[***]
Choosing and riding his faithful horse.
Walking outside, Prince Alek saw
An old man coming out of a dense forest.

Perun's[****] devotee, he followed faithfully,
Guessing this time's event,
Alek came to the elder
Who passed his youth in prayer.

"What will happen, speak, my seer!" to the follower;
"What form will my future take?
Bringing happiness to my enemies,
Will I soon be buried beneath the soil?

Speak openly! Don't hide, never worry!
Take the good horse for your speech!"
"—Shamans don't need gifts from Princes
Their fearlessness known to the people;

Their tongues free, truthful words,
Their leadership unites,

———————————

[*] Adapted to the Kazakh from Alexander Pushkin's Russian version, "Песнь о вещем Олеге" (1825).
[**] A nomadic Turkic empire in the late sixth century CE that spanned southeastern Eurasia.
[***] Slavic name for Constantinople.
[****] Highest god of the Slavic pagan mythology and god of sky, thunder, and lightning.

Dark mornings conceal you
But I see good fortune in your face.

Don't forget, remember! Words of old,
To a hero, glory and fame are riches.
Your name, valor, to humiliate your enemies,
Your shield protects your Tsargrad.

Without greed, you've been given a great fortune,
Despairing, your enemies envy you;
Earth and sea, everything under you,
An ocean's blue wave cannot beat you;

Axes, arrows, spears, daggers,
Not one will manage to harm you;
With armor around you, you won't be cut,
Your unseen sentry will suffice.

Your horse fearless and resilient;
I wonder how this feels.
'Stand!' unmoving beneath a shower of arrows
'Shoo!' ready to face a battering ram;

Warhorses inured to cold and war;
But this horse will bring your demise . . ."
The old man's words made Alek laugh,
But his thoughts and face darkened.

Saddened, he heard something unexpected,
Silent, he dismounted from his saddle.
Caressing, scratching, patting his neck,
He said goodbye to his close friend:

"Watch yourself, faithful steed, don't be hurt!
Our time together has ended, what can we do?
Take heed! Farewell! Don't forget me!
My boots won't touch your gold stirrups.

Come here, young men, grab this horse!
Lead it to my pasture!
Your blankets! Cover it with felt;
Clean, wash, feed, and take care!

Grab the best grain and oats for its meal!
Have it drink from your streams!"
They took the horse from him, Alek given another;
And many years passed after this.

~~~~~~~~~~

At a fortress, Alek celebrated,
With the guards he laughed and played,
No grief, no woe, everyone drinking,
Speaking of days past.

Then Alek remembered his horse,
Wondering: "Is it in good health? And where?
Still at your top speed?
No holding back?" He grew tired.

Going around, asking about his horse,
A man standing, "Great king!
It has been on a great hill a long time;
Your horse rests in peace."

Hearing this, Alek looked down,
He thought: "Saying nonsense, what did that old man eat?!
Sly shaman! Liar, wicked man,
You took my horse for nothing."

To see the horse's bones,
Taking Igor and his guests,
Leaving the palace, Prince Alek came,
Going along the Dnepr basin.
~~~~~~~~~~

Dried bones on top of the hill,
Grass blowing in the wind.
Buried in sand, rain washing bones within
Alek walked among them.

Slowed, feet placed, he approached the skull,
Speaking to his lost friend:
"Lie down, my friend! You left the world before me,
 God not minding your years.

It's fate that you weren't slaughtered for food.
Your blood not soiling the ground.
'Your death from your horse,' the man lied,
Did the old man scare me with this skull?!"

Unnoticed, from within the horse's skull,
A black snake cut towards the prince.
Twisting around his leg, biting hard,
A sound came from the man, and his soul escaped . . .

The people grieved for Alek in tears
After his death, but tears couldn't bring him back.
A funeral on the Dnepr's beach,
The mourners drinking with foam in cups.

Olga and the new king Igor stood above the hill:
Feasted with the army around them:
Speaking about days of old,
Cups clanging in toasts . . .

~~~~~~~~~~~
~~~~~~~~~~~

Балықшы мен Балық

Теңіздің жағасында кемпір мен шал
Тұрыбды отыз үш жыл нақ дәлме дәл.
Күн көрген бишаралар балық аулаб,
Болмабды төрт түліктен ырымға мал.

Үсті шым, асты шұңқыр жерден жырған,
Баспана мекенінің сіқы тұрған.
Бала жоқ қолғанатдық екеуінде,
Иіріб кемпір жібін, шал ау құрған.

Бір күні шал апарыб ауын салды;
Балық жоқ ауға оралған балдырды алды.
Салғанда жана ауын екінші рет,
Теңізге бітетін бір шөб оралды.

Тағы да үшінші рет ауын салыб,
Сүйретіб, шығарды бір алтын балық.
Шал байғұс өз көзіне өзі сенбей,
Аңырайыб тұрды біраз аң-таң қалыб.

Жарқыраб үсті-басы, оттай жаныб
Адамша сөз сөйлейді алтын балық:
«Жанымды бір шыбындай қи, ақсақал!
Бар болса не хажетің менен алыб».

Шал сасыб, абдырайды, есі кетіб,
Балық деб, бұ неғылған, тілге жетік?!
Керемет мұндай сірә көрген емес,
Ау салыб отыз үш жыл кәсіб етіб.

Ойланыб: «Тегін емес балық» дейді,
Қалмайын киесіне алыб, дейді;
«Һәш нәрсең керек емес жолың болсын,
Сайран ет теңізіңде барыб» дейді.

Балықты жіберді де, үйге қайтды,
Не ғажаб көргенінің бәрін айтды.
«Жібердім еш нәрсе алмай», деген соң-ақ,
Кемпірі шалға көзін бажырайтды:

«Ақымақ!» дейді: «Алжыған кеткен есің:
Былжыраб айтыб тұрсын, сөз деб несін?
Жаңа астау тым болмаса, алсаң едің,
Астаудың жарылғанын білмеймісін?»

Балыққа шал жөнелді жолықпаққа:
Ыдыска астау алыб молықпаққа.
Жыбырлаб, сұудың беті шимайланыб,
Балық кеб: «Не айтасың?» деді қартқа.

Шал айтды, қол қусырыб, тағзым етіб:
«Кемпірім ұрысыб, әбден мазам кетіб,
Жаңа астау сұрайын деб келдім, тақсыр!
Жарамсыз астаумыз, жарык-кетік».

«Қайғырма!» Балық айтды: «үйіңе бар!
Сол болса бар жұмысын, оның болар!»
Қуаныб, шал үйіне қайтыб келсе,
Бір астау әп-әдемі жатыр дайар.

Ұрсады кемпір шалға келісімен:
(Сақтасын долы қатын перісінен!)
«Алыбсың астау сұраб, ақылы жоқ.
Айырылған, ақымақ шал» дейді, есінен!

Деб ұрысты: «Миы ашыған, құу көксақал!
Астауда қызыққандай, қанша еді мал?

Қуаныб құу астауға келген несі!
Көб нәрсе әкелібсін, адырағал!
Үйіңнің үстіндегі сиқы мынау!
Балықдан барыб, тәуір үй сұраб ал!»

Тағыда шал жөнелді теңіз жаққа:
Балыққа, арыз айтыб, мұң шақбаққа
Бұзылыб судың түсі лайланыб
Балық кеб: «Не айтасың?» дейді қартқа.

Шал айтды қол қусырыб, тағзым етіб,
«Бәлеге қалдым, тақсыр! Мазам кетіб.
Үй алмай, астау алдың алжыған деб,
Барады сүйегімнен сөккені өтіб».

Арызын ақсақалдың қабыл алыб,
«Қайғырма! Үйіңе қайт!» деді балық . . .
Орнында лашығының ағаш үй тұр,
Келеді шал құуаныб, таңырқаныб.

Салган үй салтанатты сәніменен;
Бойаған, ойұулаған мәніменен;
Сайраган бақшасында түрлі құсдар,
Келтірер көңіл хошын әніменен;

Асылыб терезеге кемпір тұрыб,
Ұрсады келісімен шалға ақырыб:
«Балықтан барыбсың да үй алыбсың,
Ахмак, мыйың ашыб, кеткен шіріб.

Ізіңмен үйге кірмей, қайт балыққа!
Қадірсіз мұжық деген ат хальққа.
Айтбасқа карашекпен қатыны деб,
Ақсүйек етсін мені, айт балыққа!»

Балыққа шал келеді қайтыб тағы,
Кемпірдің мұн-мүддесін айтыб тағы.
Тағзыммен қол қусырыб арыз айтыб,
«Азабды келдім деді, тартыб тағы».

«Қайғырма!» Балық айтды, «болар» дейді;
«Ақсүйек дәрежесі қонар» деді . . .
Қатыны қайтыб келсе, болған ханым,
Қасына шал қалайша жолар енді?

Биік үй салтанатты, сәнді түрі,
Бері мол, бәрі байлық, бәрі ірі;
Үстіне неше түрлі асыл кииб,
Паңсыныб сыртқы есікте тұр кемпірі;

Қолында толған өңшең алтын жүзік,
Зүмрет, березелі бар білезік;
Үстінде қамзол ішік, тысы қамқа,
Меруерт омырауы қойған тізіб;

Айақта сақтианнан ойұулы етік;
Бұрынғы мұжықтығы естен кетіб,
Жұмсаб тұр біріне ұрсыб, бірін ұрыб,
Ақырыб малайларға әмір етіб.

Шал келіб: «Сәлем бердік, ханым!» деді,
«Ризалық табды ма, енді жаның?» деді.
Жаратбай шалдың сөзін, кемпірі ұрсыб
«Әдебсіз, ақылы жоқ, жарым» деді.
«Ат бақсын, ат қораға апарыңдар!
Мұжықтың мына біреу шалын» деді . . .

~~~~~~~~~~

Қанағат болды десек етер шағы,
Құтырды, өскен сайын кемпір бағы;
Өткен соң бірер жұма, шақыртады,
Балыққа жібермекке шалды тағы.

Айтады: «Қазір жылдам бар, балыққа!
Жеткен жоқ жаным әлі ризалыққа.
Ақсүйек дәрежесін азсынамын,
Падша етсін, мені дереу бір халыққа!»
~~~~~~~~~~

Шал айтды: «Құтырдың ба? Түзу ме есің?
Болмасын асташылық, мұның кесір!
Білмейсің іс ретін, сөз мәнісін,
Жұрт күлер: қор болған деб бахыт, есіл!»

Бұл сөзге кемпір қатты ашуланыб,
Жіберді шалды жаққа салыб-салыб.
– Қалайша маған қарсы сөз айтасың?
Сен мұжық мен ақсүйек қой деб – таныб!

Сөз айтар шалда хәл жоқ, жөнеледі.
Қарайыб теңіз беті түнереді:
Шақырған шал дауысына балық келіб,
«Ақсақал, не айтасың? Сөйле!» деді.

Шал айтды: «Өлдім әбден тынышым кетіб;
Тайанды жындануға кемпір, жетіб.
Ақсүйек дәрежесін азсынамын,
Бір жұртқа қойсын, деді, падша етіб».

«Қайғырма!» Балық сөйлеб «Кәрім!» деді,
«Істермін айтқанындай бәрін» деді,
«Жүргізіб жұртқа, әмірін мейілінше,
Айбынды болар падша жарың», деді.

Шал қайтса, салтанатты сарайлар тұр;
Ішінде сарайлардың кемпірі отыр;
Асыныб айбалтасын, есіктерде
Күзетші, түсі сұуық, малайлар тұр;

Жарқыраб, алтын кииб, оттай жаныб,
Падшасыб кемпір отыр, ызғарланыб;
Ақсүйек өңшең бекзад қызметінде,
Ішкізіб арақ-шараб, азабданыб.

Билетбей, шалға бойы, буын құрыб
Сарайға шал сескеніб келді кіріб,

Бас ұрыб кемпірінің айағына:
«Болды ма жаның риза?» деді тұрыб.

Есіркеу кемпірде жоқ, шалын айаб;
Адам деб, елеб оған қарамай-ақ;
Деб еді: «Шығарыңдар!» Сол-ақ екен –
Жұдырық жан-жағынан жауды тайақ.

Желкелеб, сүйреб жұлқыб жұлмалайды,
Ағына сақалының кім қарайды?
«Ақымақ, әдебі жоқ, алжыған құл!»
Кірлейсің айағыңмен, деб, сарайды.

Жұрт күліб, шал екенсің, деді жарым.
Ақылың кем болған соң кімге обалың?
«Болмаса өзің шанаң, отырма» деб
Бұрынғы айтбаб па еді мақалдарын?

Бір-екі мұнан кейін жұма өтді.
Тілейтін жаңа тойат кезі жетті.
Қызығы падшалықтың тозды жылдам;
Жарлық қыб, кемпір падша шалды іздетті.

Шалды айдаб, алыб келді дірдектетіб;
Байғұстың түсі қашқан, өңі кетіб.
Үстінде алтын тақтың кемпір падша
Табсырды шалға жұмыс, әмір етіб.

«Бек тығыз бұйырамын саған» деді:
«Сөз қатсаң, жыртылады жағаң» деді,
«Мақсатым сұуды билеб, сұуда тұрмақ:
Балыққа айт, менен көб-көб сәлем» деді,
«Қаратыб теңіздерді қол астыма,
Шабарман болсын өзі маған», деді.

Әлді жоқ сөз қайырар, шал кетеді.
Қорыққаннан жылдам жүріб, тез жетеді.
Қара бұлт, қара дауыл толқынды айдаб;
Сапырыб теңіз сұуын, желдетеді.

Балықты шақырыб шал, сөзін айтды
Жұмыстың тығыздығын, тезін айтды;
Кемпірдің сұрағанын естіб балық,
Бір соғыб сұуды бетке, кейін қайтды.

Балықтан жауаб күтіб тұрыб-тұрыб,
Шал қайтды кешке жақын, әлі құрыб.
Көре алмай салтанатты сарайларды,
Көз салды жан жағына мойнын бұрыб.

Қараса, лашығында кемпірі отыр;
Байағы жарық астау жырық-жырық;
Түсіріб таз кебіне бір-ақ күнде,
Қойыбды құу қақбасты Хұдай ұрыб.

The Fisherman and the Fish[*]

On the sea's coast lived an old couple
Married for thirty-three years on the day.
They saw many poor days catching fish,
Without any meat from the four animals.[**]

Grass above, a hole in the ground,
They called this place their home.
No children to help the pair,
The old woman spun thread, the old man fished.

One day the old man cast his line;
Catching no fish but slime and algae.
Cast for a second time,
Wrapped in the ocean's grass.

On the third try the old man caught something,
Pulling out a single golden fish.
The poor old man couldn't believe his eyes,
Dumbstruck, he stood, puzzled.

Glittered from top to bottom, flickering like flame,
The golden fish spoke words of man:
"Mercy on my soul, greybeard!
What is your wish you'd take from me?"

---

[*]   Adapted to the Kazakh from Alexander Pushkin's Russian version, "Сказка о рыбаке и рыбке" (1835).
[**]   The four animals of traditional Kazakh meals include sheep, camel, cow, and horse.

The old man was confused, taken, excited,
"The fish spoke, what is it, it's able to talk?!"
Something this incredible never seen,
Casting line in all his thirty-three years of fishing.

He thought: "This is not an ordinary fish,
But a sacred kind;
I don't need anything from you, safe travels,
Have fun in your ocean," he said.

Fish released, he returned to the house,
Speaking all about the wonder of the day.
"I sent him without taking anything," he said finally,
The old woman's eyes glared.

"I can't believe it!" she said. "Are you senile?
Speaking like this, why are you telling me?
No new basin, you could have taken,
Did you forget your basin has split?"

The old man set out to find the fish again:
To grow their wares with a basin.
Moving, the water's face scribbled,
The fish came: "What do you say?" he asked the old man.

The old man spoke, hands twisted, bowing low:
"My wife scolded me, my peace gone,
I came to ask for a new basin, my lord!
Ours is unfit, split, and broken."

"Don't grieve!" The fish said, "Go home!
If it's the only thing you want, it will be there!"
Delighted, the old man returned,
A beautiful new basin standing before him.

The angry wife resolved:
(Mind the rageful women, fairies!)
"You asked for the basin, you idiot.
You've lost your mind you stupid old man."

She argued: "Your mind's blank, greybeard!
This wonderful basin, for how many animals?

Why are you happy just for a basin here!
You've brought lots of things, you bastard!
And the house still looks like this!
Go to the fish, ask for a decent home!"

Again the old man went to the shore:
Petitioned the fish, telling him his sadness,
The water breaking and stirring,
It came: "What will you say?" he said to the old man.

The old man twisted his hands, bowing low,
"I'm struggling, majesty! No peace for me.
I didn't take the house, but a basin, called 'senile,'
My wife's words hurt me."

Accepting the old man's complaint,
"Don't worry! Go back to your house!" said the fish . . .
A wooden house standing in place of the shack,
The old man arriving amazed.

A magnificent home stood luxurious;
Painted, decorated, and beautiful;
Birds sang in the orchard,
Happiness sung in melodies;

The old woman hung out the window.
When he returned, she shouted to her husband:
"You went to the fish and got just a home,
Idiot, empty head, rotten brain.

Don't come in, go back to the fish!
Worthless peasant, people call you.
Don't let them call me a peasant's wife," she said,
"I need noble blood, tell the fish!'"

---

*   Literally "white bone." Used in some Turkic language communities of medieval Central
    Asia indicating direct lineage from the Chingissid, Kazakh Khan, or noble blood line.

The old man came back to the fish,
Repeating his wife's complaint again.
With a low bow and twisted hands,
"I suffered again," he grumbled.

"Don't fret!" the fish said, "It will be done;
Noble blood and rank will be yours," it said . . .
He came again to his wife, now a noble,
How could the old man approach her?

In the giant palace, elegant,
All was well, wealthy, everything massive;
Adorned with various gemstones,
Boastful, she stood at the gates and met the old man;

On her hand were many gold rings,
Emeralds, diamonds on her bracelet;
Wearing an īshīk,* fine leathers,
Pearls draped around her neck;

On her legs she wore horsehide boots;
Her peasant status long gone,
Now leading by hitting, shouting,
Yelling, and commanding her servants.

The old man came: "Hello, my lady!
Are you satisfied now, your soul?"
Disapproving of the old man's words, she fought.
"Tactless, mindless, fool," she said.
"Drag him to the barn, have him feed the horse!
Just an old peasant," she said . . .

~~~~~~~~~~~

---

*   Traditional Kazakh fur-lined outerwear.
~~~~~~~~~~~

Thinking she'd be satisfied in her state,
Her madness rising with her wealth;
After one week, she called him,
To send the old man to the fish again.

"Fast now, go fish!
I'm still not gratified.
Class and status are insufficient,
Make me a queen, a leader of the people!"

"Are you crazy? Are you thinking straight?
Don't be this greedy, this evil!
You don't know the work, the meaning of words,
People will laugh: You wasted happiness for arrogance!"

These words infuriated the old woman,
Hitting the old man again and again.
"—How dare you speak to me that way?
You are a peasant, I'm royalty—you know better!"

The old man couldn't reply; he left.
The surface of the sea becoming cloudy:
Hearing the sounds of the old man, the fish came,
"Old man, what do you say? Speak!"

The old man said: "I've died in my silence;
My wife going mad, nearing it.
'My noble blood and rank now inadequate,
I want to be made a people's queen,' she said."

"Don't fear!" said the fish. "My old man!
I'll do everything you asked," it said,
"To rule the people, order her desires,
She will become a powerful queen."

The old man returned to the palace,
His wife seated within;

Axes mounted on the doors,
Guards, looking stoic, servants standing;

Sparkling, wearing gold, shining like flame,
The queen wife sat menacing;
Nobility of royal blood and class,
Now serving alcohol and wine, drinking.

Powerless, the old man losing his status,
He went to the palace afraid to enter,
Bowing to his wife:
"Is your soul satisfied?" he asked.

She had no sympathy for the old man's pleas;
Not seeing him as a person;
"Get him out of here!" she said,
The old man dragged by wrists everywhere.

Beating, dragging, jerking, wrestling,
Who saw the white of his beard?
"Idiot, simple, senile fool!
Your feet have dirtied the palace!"

The people laughed at the old man, the fool.
"Who can you blame for your stupidity?
'If the sled isn't yours, don't sit.'
Didn't the old proverb say this?"

One, two weeks like this passed.
But the time for a new pleasure came.
The intrigue of the kingdom quickly waned;
The old queen ordered to find the old man.

He was dragged shivering from the cold;
His face flushed, his color leaving him.
Above him on the golden throne sat the old queen,
Entrusting the old man to work, doing her bidding.

"You're dim to my commands," she said.
"If you say anything, your collar will be torn,
My goal is to rule the water, to live in it;
Tell the fish, with many 'hello's," she said,
"All the seas under my rule,
The fish could be my messenger."

Powerless to speak, the old man left.
Walking fast out of fear, he arrived quickly.
Dark clouds and storm called the waves;
Stirring the seawater, gusting.

The old man called for the fish, told him
The work is urgent, must be done soon;
The fish hearing his wife's question,
One splash of the water, the fish left.

Awaiting the fish's answer a long time,
The old man returned in the evening, powerless.
Unable to see the splendor of the palace,
Eyes seeing what was near beneath his bent neck.

He looked, the old woman sitting in the shack;
The trough split in half, filled of holes;
She'd fallen in only a single day,
This rotten person punished by God.

Алтын Әтеш

Беріде емес әріде,
Пәлен жұртдың жерінде,
     Болған жақсы хан Дадан.
Талай көріб хауібді,
Талай жұртты шауыбды,
     Жасында боб бек мазақ.

Жас жеткен соң жабығыб,
Аттаныстан жалығыб,
     Жай жатұуға ойлабды.

Кәрі ханды қажалаб,
Енді өзгелер, мазалаб,
     Жай жатқызыб қоймабды.

Жаудан Дадан жерлерін,
Қорғамаққа елдерін,
     Һәман тұтды көб әскер.
Қолбасылар қалғымас,
Тұс-тұсынан шықты қас,
     Қайсысына жетісер?

Оңнан күтсе, жау солда;
Қырдан күтсе, жау сұуда;
     Арқадан да, Құбыладан;
Жан жағынан жау ұрды,
Жылаб-жылаб жіберді
     Ызасынан хан Дадан.

Қатты күйді, қайғырды;
Хан ұйқыдан айырылды;
    Һаман қауіф-қатерде.
Ойлаб, ойлаб қарайды:
Не қылсам деб жарайды?
    Білмейді не етерге.

Безген, ат боб, белінен,
Һәр нәпсінің желінен,
    Бар екен бір данышпан,
Жұлдыз санаб қарайтын,
Сонан ақыл сұрайтын
    Сасқан йаки адасқан.

Арнаб кісі шабдырыб,
Көб-көб сәлем айтдырыб,
    Шақыртады хан Дадан
Шақырғанға бұ барды;
Алтын әтеш шығарды,
    Аузын шешіб дорбадан.

Ханға тұрыб сөйлейді;
Сөйлегенде бүй дейді:
    «Мынау алтын әтешім;
Қондыр сырық басына!
Қой сарайың қасына!
    Болар мықты күзетшің.

Бұл отырса тыб-тыныш,
Жоқ һеш жерде қорқыныш.
    Қатер болса бір жақта,
(Соғыс па иә әлдене?
Болсын мейлі не бәле)
    Қараб әтеш сол жаққа,

Күдірейіб дауыстар:
Ол дегені «Хауіб бар!»
    Риза болыб, айтар хан:

«Бұйым, алтын күміс бе?
Басқа мүдде, жұмыс ба?
        Тауаныңды қайтарман.

Сенен немді айармын!
Қашан болса, дайармын,
        Не сұрасаң беруге.
Не десең де еткізіб,
Не мүддеңе жеткізіб,
        Өз көңілімдей көруге».

~~~~~~~~~~

Биік сырық басында,
Хан сарайы қасында,
        Қарауылдаб халықды,
Қатер болса, жұлқыныб,
Солай қарай ұмтылыб,
        Әтеш айқай салыбды.

«Кіри-ку-ку, жат, ханым!
Жатыб жұртды бақ, ханым!»
        Дадан ісін асырды:
Жауын ерте көрген соң,
Ұрыб, сыйын берген соң,
        Жау тыйылды, басылды.

Бір жыл өтті, екі жыл;
Табды рахат жұрт дамыл;
        Әтеш отыр жай, тыныш.
Бір күн ұйықтаб хан жатды.
Сер әскер кеб, ойатды,
        Бар деб бәле – қорқыныш.

Хан аша алмай ұйқысын,
«Не бәле бар? Не қысым?»
        Дейді отырыб есінеб.
~~~~~~~~~~

Жауаб берді сер әскер:
«Әтеш көрген бар қатер;
    Жұрт хауібде, түйсініб».

Хан қараса әйнекден;
Әтеш отыр әндеткен;
    Күншығысқа қарабды.
«Не тұрыс бар? Жүрүуге!
Жылдам атқа мінүуге!
    Алыб қарұу-жарақды!»

Хан ғәскерін айдайды,
Үлкен ұлын сайлайды,
    Бастық етіб үстінен.
Әтеш тағы жай тыныш,
Хауіб-қатер, қорқыныш
    Шықды жұртдың есінен.

Қол шыққалы жеті күн,
Әскерден жоқ хабар-үн:
    Ашықды ма? Тоқба әлі?
Жеткен жоқба? Жетді ме?
Жау жатыр ма? Кетді ме?
    Соғысды ма? Жоқ ба әлі?

Міне, әтеш бақырды:
Хан өзге қол шақырды;
    Кіші ұлына бастатды.
Күншығысқа бет беріб,
Қарұу, қабшық бөктеріб,
    Қосын артыб, қол тартды.

Әтеш тыныш, қылмыс жоқ;
Әскерден түк дыбыс жоқ.
    Тағы өтеді жеті күн.
Жұрт айырылды сауықдан,
Ел жайғасбай қауыбдан,
    Әтеш тағы берді үн.

Үшінші қол шақырыб;
Тастайындай жапырыб,
    Құтты болғай деб қадам,
Күн шығысқа жол алыб,
Азық-түлік мол алыб,
    Шықды өзі хан Дадан.

Күн-түн демей, қол жүріб;
Бітті әбден болдырыб,
    Һешбір белгі жолда жоқ.
Мола да жоқ, көр де жоқ,
Салық салған жер де жоқ,
    Соғыс да жоқ, қол да жоқ.

«Бұ не хикмет! Не ғажаб!»
Дейді Дадан ойға қаб.
    Жетінші күн батыр хан,
Қолды жиын жүргізіб,
Тау ішіне кіргізіб,
    Көрді жібек шатыр хан.

Маңайында ел де жоқ;
Ызыңдаған жел де жоқ;
    Жалғыз ғана сол шатыр.
Өзекдерде, ойларда,
Жыбырлаған қойлардай,
    Қырыб салған қол жатыр.

Хан шатырға кірмекке,
Бұ не ғажаб білмекке,
    Жылдамрақ жүреді.
Хан алдында екі ұлы,
Жан шошитын бар сыны,
    Жатқандарын көреді.
Бір біріне қылышды
Сұғыб, табқан тынышды;
    Сауыт, қалқан жоқ бәрі.

Жапырылыб жаншылған,
Қара қанға малшынған,
      Шөбді жеб түр атдары.

«Екі азамат сұлтаным!
Екі лашын-сұңқарым!
      Ауға түскен, алданған.
Маған күйік! Маған дерт!
Маған өлім! Маған мерт!»
      Деб жылады хан Дадан.

Хан жыласа, қалар ма?
Ерген жасақ олар да
      Еңіресді, жыласды.
Тау күрсініб, күңіреніб,
Ой ыңылдаб, ыңыраныб,
      Бәрі бірге ұласды.

Сонда шатыр ашылыб,
Нұры күндей шашылыб,
      Шамаһанды билеген,
Нөкері жоқ, жаб-жалғыз
Шыға келіб патша қыз,
      Ұшырасды ханменен.

Қуыршаққа қуанған,
Балаларша уанған,
      Жылағанын хан қойды.
Сыландаған, сызылыб,
Қызға көңіл бұзылыб,
      Бөлмей, жармай, берді ойды.

Керіле басыб, кекекдеб,
Ханды қолдан жетектеб,
      Қыз шатырға апкетді.
Дастарханды жайады;
Түрлі тағам қойады;
      Көрсетеді құрметді.

Әбден сыйлаб бағады;
Барша төсек салады,
	Тынықсын деб жол шеккен . . .
Бір жұмадай тойлар хан,
Басқаны жоқ ойлар хан,
	Басы айналған, ерік кеткен . . .

~~~~~~~~~~

Міне, қолын, қосын аб,
Қызды өзіне қосыб аб,
	Кейін қарай хан басты.
Келмей жатыб алдынан:
Пәлен екен деб пәлен –
	Түрлі лақаб, сөз қашды.

Тайанғанда қалаға,
Дұулаб, шұулаб далаға,
	Хан алдынан ел шықды.
Жұрт жүгірер артынан;
Хан, сағынған халқынан,
	Алар сәлем, құлдықды.

Көб ішінен көреді:
Біреу сәлем береді;
	Ақ бөркі бар басында;
Ет жоқ, ұрты сұуалған,
Сақал, мұрты құуарған,
	Қара қыл жоқ шашында.

Шал сәлемін хан алыб,
Кәрі досын тез таныб,
	«Жақын кел» деб шақырды.
Дейді: «Аманба? Қарт бабам!
Не қосасың? Айт, бабам!
	Данышпаным, ақылды»
~~~~~~~~~~

Шал айтады: «Хан Дадан!
Бар-ды айтқан уағдаң:
    Тілегімді берүуге;
Не десем де еткізіб,
Ризалыққа жеткізіб,
    Өз көңіліңдей көрүуге.

Ақы алатын күн жетті,
Мойныңдағы міндетті
    Өте, бүгін қарызды.
Сүйсең көңілім тынұуын,
Бер, Шамаһан сұлұуын!
    Қабыл ет, хан, арызды!»

Хан таңданды бұл іске;
Ойдағы жоқ ұлы іске.
    Шалға айтды: «Сен несің?
Пері енді ме, түсіңе!
Жын кірді ме, ішіңе?
    Алжастың ба, бар ма есің?

Мен саған шын қарыздар:
Қарызда да шама бар –
    Қыз ол саған не қажет?
Қой, шалым, тым зор тұтба!
Мен кім! Оны ұмытба!
    Міндетден бар зор міндет.

Сұра менен қазына!
Қараман көб-азына.
    Шен десең, шен беремін.
Ат қала да, атымды ал!
Зат қала да, затымды ал!
    Ел жарымын һәм беремін».

«Керек емес» деді шал:
Елің, шенің, бұйым, мал.
    Берсең, маған қызды бер!

«Түф!» деб жерге түкіріб!
Хан айтады жекіріб,
        (Қысылғаннан шықды тер)

«Құураған шал! Сый алмай,
Қыз сұрайсың ұйалмай,
        Соққан сені захмет.
Түк нәрсе де бермеймін,
Түк есебді көрмеймін.
        Сау тұрғанда, жоғал! Кет!»

Ханға жауаб қайырыб,
Таласұуға бой ұрыб,
        Шал айтқанша қамданыб . . .
Хан асамен маңдайға
«Таласатын қандай? Мә!»
        Деб жіберді бір салыб.

Етбетінен шал түсді;
Тәннен безіб жаны ұшды;
        Қыз «хы-хы-хы! Ха-ха-ха!»
Қорықпайды екен обалдан.
Күлген болды һәм Дадан.
        Жұрт ренжүу, хан хафа.

Не тұрыс бар далада?
Хан кіреді қалаға,
        Жұрт көшеге толады;
Сырығынан түсіб кеб,
Алтын әтеш ұшыб кеб,
        Хан басына қонады;

Тұмсығымен шабды да,
Ханның миын шақды да,
        Әтеш кетті асбанға;
Арбасынан хан ұшды;
Кеудесінен жан ұшды;
        Қалды барша жұрт таңға.

Ғайыб болды, қыз кетді.
Сөз айағы һәм жетті
    Істеу шабан, айтұу тез;
Ертегінің шыны аз;
Шыны аздың құны аз;
    Жанаб айтқан жай бір сөз.

Not near, but far,
In a place of other people,
    There was a great king Dadan.
He saw lots of danger,
Attacking many peoples,
    Mocked in his youth.

Youth long gone, withered,
His fame now mundane,
    He thought of lying around.
The old king worn,
But others, disturbing him,
    Wouldn't let him rest.

Against enemies, Dadan's lands,
And their nations,
    Soldiers always standing by.
Generals couldn't rest,
Enemies all around,
    Who could handle it?

---

* Adapted to the Kazakh from Alexander Pushkin's Russian version, "Сказка о золотом петушке" (1835).

If from the right, enemies to the left;
If from the country, enemies from the sea;
    From the rear, from Kobula;[*]
Striking from every side,
Unable to stop his tears,
    Dadan's frustration grew.

His state of despair, sadness;
The king's sleep disturbed;
    Always in grave danger.
Thinking through ideas:
What could I possibly do?
    He didn't know what he could.

Abandoned, exhausted from his place,
Every gust of desire,
    A single wise person,
He saw counting the stars,
Then asked for advice,
    Confused and mistaken.

He sent people on his behalf,
Many 'hello's spoken,
    King Dadan invited him
And the wise man arrived;
He presented a golden rooster,
    Opened from the mouth of a bag.

The wise man spoke to the king;
Speaking this way:
    "This is my golden rooster;
Install it at the head of a spire!
Place it near the palace!
    It will be your strongest guard.

---

[*]   A mountain in the Ukrainian Carpathians.

When it is quietest,
There is nothing to fear.
    If danger on one side,
(Could it be war?
Another misfortune?)
    The rooster watching that,

It'll make its noise:
'There's danger!'"
    Satisfied, the king said:
"My gift, shall it be gold? Silver?
A favor, a deed?
    Your strength will not return.

What I wouldn't give you!
When possible, I'm prepared,
    Whatever you want, I'll give.
Whatever you say, I'll do,
Whatever your aims, I'll follow,
    To see to them as if my own."

~~~~~~~~~~~

On top of a large post,
Near the king's palace,
    Guarding the people,
If danger, rushing forward,
Reaching toward,
    The rooster cried.

"Cock-a-doodle-doo, my king!
Defend the people, my king!"
    Dadan succeeded:
After seeing the enemy early,
Striking, then giving gifts,
    Foes suppressed and weighed upon.
~~~~~~~~~~~

A year passed, another;
People finding pleasure in rest;
    The rooster calmed, quieted.
One day the king slept.
A brave soldier came, awoke,
    A misfortune—dread.

The king slow to rise,
"What trouble is there? What force?"
    He said yawning.
The brave soldier answered:
"The rooster has seen danger;
    It feels the people threatened."

The king looked from the window;
The rooster crooned;
    Looking to the east.
"What's there? Go on!
I'll go quick to my horse!
    Arm yourselves!"

The king's soldier drove on,
The large son chosen,
    The boss working above.
The rooster silent once more,

Danger, misfortune, fear,
    Left the people's minds.

The seventh day letting go,
No word returned from the soldier:
    Did they starve? Well-fed?
Not make it? Arrive?
Caught by an enemy? Fled?
    In battle? Or not?

Here, the rooster shouted:
The king called for reinforcements;
     The smallest brother began.
Approaching the east,
Weapons tied in a small bag,
     Tent set, fastened.

The rooster quiet, no crimes;
Not a sound from the soldiers.
     Another seven days passed.
The people lost their mood,
The country anxious from fear,
     The rooster sounded once more.

The third reinforcements;
Like throwing and crushing,
     Success in their steps,
Taking the road to the east,
Taking provisions aplenty,
     King Dadan took to himself.

Day and night they walked,
Exhausted from everything,
     Not one mark on the road,
Not a cemetery was seen,
No station to pay a tax,
     No war, no soldiers.

"What wisdom! What miracle!"
Said Dadan with a thought.
     On the seventh day the hero king,
Gathered the soldiers,
Went into the mountain,
     Where the king saw a silk tent.

No one near;
No rustling wind;
     Alone stood the tent.

Holes, thoughts,
As sheep twitching,
    Soldiers killed everywhere.

The king entered the tent,
To discover this miracle,
    Walking quickly.
The king saw his two sons,
Terrified of the vision,
    Lying before him.

Blades used against each other,
They stabbed, found silence;
    No armor to be seen.
Pulverized, trampled,
Grasses grazed by horses,
    Drenched in black blood.

"Two brave sultans!
Two peregrine falcons!
    Fallen into a trap, deceived.
I'm scalded! Diseased!
Doom to me! Death!"
    Cried King Dadan.

The king wept so others could.
The army followed close
    In their cries and wails.
The mountains sighing, groaning,
The valleys softly sung, moaning,
    All following each other.

Then opened the tent,
Light strewn like the sun,
    The ruler Shamahan,
Without soldiers, all alone
Came the queen,
    To meet the king.

Like delighted in a doll,
Like a child consoled,
        The weeping king stopped.
Adorned, drawn,
Emotions distracted by the queen,
        Attention undivided, unsplit, he gave his thought.

Walking softly, neck straight,
The king led by hand,
        The queen entering the tent.
Dastarqan* spread;
Different foods placed;
        Showing honor and respect.

A full setting gifted and appraised;
Entire bed prepared,
        Resting from a long journey . . .
The king celebrated a week's feast,
Without another thought,
        Within a fantasy, his freedom gone . . .

~~~~~~~~~~~

Here, taking his soldiers, his people,
Taking the queen with him,
        The king headed back home.
Before he arrived, in front of him:
Chatter, muttered, and hushed,
        Different rumors, words spoken.

Nearing the city,
A clamoring, noise from afar,
        People suddenly came before him.
The people ran from behind;
Those who missed the king
        Received greetings, deference.

---

*   A table spread with a multitude of dishes to display the host's wealth and generosity.
~~~~~~~~~~~

From the crowd:
He saw one greeting him;
    A white fur cap on his head;
Skinny, cheeks weathered,
Bearded, mustache faded,
    No black left in his hair.

An old man greets the king,
Recognizing an old friend,
    "Come closer," he called.
"Are you well? My wizened grandfather!
What's new? Speak, elder!
    Your wisdom, your sense."

The old man said, "King Dadan!
Speaking of your promise:
    My wish will be given;
Do what I say,
Bring about satisfaction,
    Treat me as you treat yourself.

The day for my gift has come,
Recognize your commitment,
    Return your debt today.
If you love my happiness,

Give me the beautiful queen Shamaḣan!
    Receive, my king, my call!"

The king was surprised by the demand;
This great one unimagined.
    To the old man, he said, "What are you?
Did a fairy enter your dreams!
Did a jinn* possess you?
    Are you senile, your wits about you?

---

*   Invisible spirits that can change forms and interfere in human affairs.

"I am still in your debt:
But there are limits to this.
        Why do you need the queen?
Stop, old friend, don't desire so much!
Who am I? Don't forget that!
        From duty there is greater duty.

"Ask for my treasure!
It doesn't matter, a lot or a little.
        If you name a rank, I'll give it.
If you want a horse, take it!
If you want anything, have it!
        A split country you'll receive."

"That's not necessary," the old man said,
"Your country, your rank, your jewelry, wealth.
        If you give me anything, give me your woman!"

"Pfff!" the king spat!
He raised his voice,
        (His skin sweating)

"Frustrating old man! You won't take gifts,
Asking for my woman without shame,
        The devil's taken your mind.
I'll give you nothing,
Nothing left to consider.
        Now disappear, or else! Get!"

Before the old man could prepare . . .
Before he could answer the king,
        Thinking his argument,
The king with staff in hand,
"You'll keep arguing? Ah!"
        Hit the old man on the forehead.

The old man collapsed;
Body abandoned, his soul flew;
    The woman cried, "Ho-ho-ho! Ha-ha-ha!"
No pity in her cries,
King Dadan faking a laugh.
    The people offended, as the king.

Why would they stay outside the city?
The king entered,
    And the people gathered;
Coming down from the post,
The golden rooster flew,
    Landing on the sovereign.

Its beak crushing
The king's skull,
    The rooster soared;
From a cart the king flew;
Spirit leaving the body;
    Everyone shocked.

Suddenly, the queen left.
Nothing left to say.
    Faster to speak than do,
Little truth in the story;
What little truth, little value;
    Coming to a close.

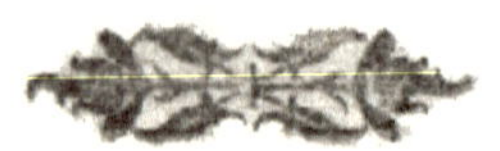

 ЛермонтоФдан[*]

Екі өзен – Кура, Арагуа ағыб келіб
Кездесіб бір-біріне сәлем беріб,
Жерінде екеуінің нақ көріскен,
Аңсаған ағайындай бауыры еріб.

Монастыр тұрұушы еді бұрын-рақ.
Өзі жоқ, бұл күнде бар орны бірақ.
Жайауға таудан шыққан көрінеді
Бағандар қақба орнында қалған құлаб.

Бұзылған шіркеудің тұр қабырғасы,
Көрінбес қазір, бірақ, онда шырақ.
Бұл күнде[**] монахтар да жоқ ішінде,
Көб үшін дұға қылғыш тілек сұраб.

Құлаған орнын қараб бағатын бір,
Жан түгіл, өлім зорға табатын бір,
Күзетші, жарымжан шал молалардың
Тасдарын сүртіб, шаңын қағатын бір.

---

[*]   Отрывок из поэми Лермонтова «Мцыри».
[**] Монах – софы.

Сөйлейді тас жазұуы өткендерін
Қайрылмай қандай дәурен кешкендерін.
Мәсәлән пәлен падша пәлен жылы
Орысқа жұртын табыс еткендерін.

~~~~~~~~~~

Бір жылы монастырға тұрған жолда
(Ішінде монахдары бар кезі онда)
Келді де орысдың бір жанаралы,
Қасында жау баласы түскен қолға,
Тифлис шаһарына өтіб кетді,
Баланы науқастанған тастаб сонда.

Шамасы бала сонда алты жасар,
Құурайдай жіб-жіңішке, нәзік, нашар;
Сықылды тау киігі жатырқағыш
Жоламай жанға жақын сырттап қашар.

Батса да дерті жанға қанша қинаб,
Сыр бермей жатды бала күшін жинаб,
Қайысбас тұқымына біткен қайрат
Шынықды дертбен қатар іште шираб.

Ауырыб жатсадағы өлім халда
Аңқылдаб шақбас дертін еш адамға
Жалғыз-ақ ишаратбен білдіреді
Мейлі шабпағанын дәм-тағамға.

Біреуі манахдардың жатсынбай-ақ,
Қарады, бақды есіркеб баланы айаб;
Емімен жаны ашыған жақындықдың,
Өлімнен аман қалды, барыб тайаб.

Әуелі жүрді бәрін бөтенсініб;
Бала боб жоқ ойнау еш жеңілшілік;
Жатырқаб жан адамға жоламасдан
Үндемей дәйім оқшау бөлек жүріб,
~~~~~~~~~~

Сағыныб туған жерін, күн шығысқа
Қойады қараб, қараб құр күрсініб.
Сонан соң жат қолында жалғыздыққа
Көрінді үйренгендей тілін біліб.

~~~~~~~~~~

Баланы шоқындырды поп бабасы;
Өскен соң манах қылмақ ер адасы;
Танысбай дүниамен талақ етіб,
Қалыбды қол табсырар уағдасы.

Бір түні жоқ боб шықды қашыб зытқан
Айнала қалың орман, тауға шыққан.
Үш күндей әуре болыб іздеб, іздеб
Үмітді үзердей боб әрең табқан.

Табдық деб жатқан жерде есін таныб,
Қайтадан манастырға келісді алыб.
Тартқандай ашдық, бейнет, дерт азабын
Бозарыб, қатты жүдеб, қалған арыб.

Ћеш кімге сұраса да түк үндемей,
Солады күннен күнге бейне гүлдей;
Өлерге тайанғанда қарт манах кеб,
Үгітдеб, «қылмысың бар, – деді, – нендей?»

Балаға шалдың сөзі болды қайрақ,
Көтеріб жерден басын, көзі жайнаб,
Қатайыб қалған бойда күшін жиыб,
Тарқатыб шерді бала айтды сайраб:

«Сен келдің, өлерде айтар сыр тыңдауға;
Ризамын, келгеніңе бұл тыңдауға;
Көкірек жеңілткенім маған жақсы,
Сөзімді керек қылса, кім тыңдауға;
~~~~~~~~~~

Қылмыс жоқ, бәһре алыб пайдаланар,
Ісім бар, айтыб өтер құр тыңдауға!
Айтұуға жан жарасын тіл жете ме?
Сала бер құлағыңды, мұң тыңдауға!

Дүниа болды маған аз-ақ серік,
Ол-дағы тұтқындықда, қамауда еріб;
Бұл түрлі тіршіліктің екеуіне
Толық бір өмір алұу сатса беріб.

Жалғыз-ақ, ұлығ тұтдым ойдың күшін;
Жалғыз-ақ, бір құмарды сақтады ішім;
Жанымды құртдай жайлаб, жегідей жеб,
Күйдіріб сол құмар-ақ бітірді ісін.

Шақырды құмар мені бұл орыннан,
Бықырсыб, пысынаған жылы орыннан.
Қатерден қан қайнайтын жерге шық деб
Өлімге тіршілігі құл орнынан.

Ой ұшды, адам құсдай, азад жаққа;
Өлім мен өмір қатар қабат жаққа;
Таулары басын бұлтқа жасыратын,
Ләззат мол тіршілікде ғажаб жаққа.

Сол құмар мен жасымнан баққан бабтаб,
Айтбастан һеш адамға ішде сақтаб.
Асыраб көз жасымен түн болғанда
Жасырын жұртдың бәрі жатқанда ұйықтаб.

Мұнымды жариа ғыб мойныма алыб,
Һешкімге жалынбаймын, кеш деб ақтаб».

~~~~~~~~~~
~~~~~~~~~~

«Жел жұлған жабырақдай ұшыб келіб,
Күн түсбес күнгірт жерде солдым семіб;
Өлімге ара тұрыб, алыб қабсың;
Қажет не? Жақсы еді ғой қалған өліб!
Тұнжыраб тұшшы жүз жоқ, өстім жалғыз,
Сопылық, бала басым күнін көріб.

Сүйікті «әкем», «шешем» дейтін сөздер,
Оны айтбай еш адамға жан не төзер?
Жүрекпен бірге туған тәтті сөзден,
Ұмытыб жат қолында дедің безер.

Жанмен бір тұуған үндер жоғалар ма?
Қарасам үлкендерге, балаларға:
Тұуысқан, үйі, ұлты, дос-жары бар,
Жоқ екен маған жақын молалар да.

Төкпейін көздің жасын дедім текке,
Ант ішіб өзімді-өзім салдым сертке:
Болсада түсі қанық, тұуғаны бір
Төсімді тайаб жақын көкірекке.

Құмардан ерте-кеш пе, шықпақ едім,
Өлетін болсам да нақ сол минөтте.
Дариға, ол қиалым баққан жастан,
Жоғалды, енді артына қайрылмастан.

Жат жерде, жау қолында жалғыз өлем,
Жетімдік, тұтқындықтан құтылмастан.»

From Lermontov

Two rivers—Kura, Aragua flow
See each other and greet
At the place where they exactly meet,
Rushing toward another like brothers.

A monastery stood there long ago.
No longer there, but its place remains.
Visible high in the mountains
Pillars collapsed from their gates.

In the broken walls of the church,
Not a single ray of light.
No longer monks to enter,
A place for many to offer prayers.

In the wreckage, one cared for it,
Not only a soul, even death couldn't find him.
An old guard protected the fallen graves,
Drying dampness and cleaning dull headstones.

He spoke to tombs, of carvings written,
How fortunes shifted long ago.
Like an old king
Giving his people to Russia.

~~~~~~~~~~

---

*　Adapted to the Kazakh from Mikhail Lermontov's Russian version, "Мцыри" (1840).
~~~~~~~~~~

One year, on the path to the monastery
(Where the monks lived within)
Came a Russian general
With a young captive, hands tied,
Bound toward Tbilisi,
But he left the ill child at the monastery.

The captive of about six years,
Thin as a reed, weak, frail;
Skittish like a mountain goat
Never close to people, running away.

How sunk in sickness, tormented soul,
Never showing signs of recovery.
His stubbornness, his power, in his blood
Resolved despite the swirling illness within.

Even if close to death
He would never cry to another.
With only small signs showing
No appetite for food.

One monk didn't shy away,
Took care, felt for, pitied the boy;
With a cure of compassion,
Pulled him from death, braced him.

At first, afraid of near strangers;
The boy couldn't play as a child;
Too shy to be with others,
Always silent, walking separately.
Homesick, he turned to the east,
Watching carefully, longing.
In time he became used to the loneliness
Of strangers and adapted to this life.

~~~~~~~~~~~
~~~~~~~~~~~

The child was converted;
Wanting him to grow into a monk, not a man,
Not knowing the world, divorced from it,
Left a promise entrusted.

One night, he fled without a sound
Through the forest, to the mountains.
Three days they wasted searching, searching,
Almost losing hope, but with toil, they found him.

Found him lying on the ground,
Taking him again to the monastery.
Starved, struggling, ill once more,
Paled, thin and weak, sickened.

No one could muster a sound,
Day by day wilting like a flower;
Near death, an elder monk came to him,
In support, "Your guilt?" he said, "What is it?"

The old man's words sharpened the boy,
Raising his head, eyes sparkling,
Stiffened, but soon gathering strength,
Unwound his sorrows, and the boy spoke:

"You came for me to confess on death's edge;
I'm pleased for you to hear my confession;
It's good to lighten my heart,
If my words must be heard;

No wrongdoing from which I could learn from,
I have words that will be said just for you!
Will my speech convey my soul?
Lend your ear for a sad tale!

The world was unfriendly,
Stuck in captivity, following in prison;
If I could trade for a full life,
These two existences, I would.

I admired only the power of ideas;
A single passion preserved inside;
My soul eaten by worms,
Burned from within by my longing.

Passion pulling me from this place,
Dirty, dampened from this warmth.
My blood boiled from danger of leaving here
Its existence, a slave of death.

An idea flew, like a bird, to freedom;
Death and life in line, layered;
Peaks of mountains hidden behind clouds,
Pleasure of being in beauty.

That passion I tended in my youth,
Never telling a soul what I kept inside.
Feeding my tears in the night,
Hidden while everyone slept.

I can't risk making this known,
I beg to no one, saying it's too late."

~~~~~~~~~~

"The wind plucked me flying like a leaf,
Withering in the place without sunlight,
Protecting from death, you saved me;
Why? I'm better off dead!
Frowning from no warmth, I grew up alone,
Religious, surviving as a child.

The lovely 'father,' 'mother' words,
Spoken to no one, who could bear it?
Sweet words born from the heart,
Forgetting them in this foreign land.
~~~~~~~~~~

Will the song born of our soul vanish?
If I saw the adults, to the children:
There is birth, womb, nation, friends,
Not even graves close to me.

Stopping my pointless tears,
A vow sworn to myself:
If the dream is deep, a relative
Hold me chest to chest.

Sooner or later, I'd leave my passion,
Even if I died at that exact minute.
Alas, my dream I tended,
Gone, now won't look back at me.

There, by my enemy's hands, I'll die alone,
Orphaned, captive, and everything but free."

www.ingramcontent.com/pod-product-compliance
Lightning Source LLC
Chambersburg PA
CBHW031047310726
48969CB00007B/2150